OUTMATCHED WITCH

MISS MATCHED MIDLIFE DATING AGENCY
BOOK THREE

DEANNA CHASE

Bayou Moon Press, LLC

www.deannachase.com

Printed in the United States of America

ABOUT THIS BOOK

A paranormal women's fiction novel

Just as Marion Matched's relationship is heating up and her business is exploding with clients, her estranged sister, Charlotte, shows up after accidentally unleashing an unlawful curse on all the men down at the local bar. With treatment resistant acne and erectile dysfunction the new norm for most of the men in town, matchmaking in Premonition Pointe has more challenges than ever. Now, with her sister living with her, Marion not only has to come to terms with their strained relationship, but she needs to help Charlotte find a way to reverse the curse before her business goes under or the law comes knocking.

When it turns out there's something more evil lurking than just an accidental curse, the two sisters end up facing past traumas that threaten to break them both. The lives they've started to build in Premonition Pointe are on the line, and now they'll have to learn to work together or else they face losing everything...including their new sisterly bond that neither ever saw coming.

CHAPTER 1

*T*he little brown and black mini chihuahua darted across my house into the dining room, straight toward my boyfriend, Jax, her high-pitched bark piercing my eardrums.

"Minx, baby," Charlotte, my red-headed half sister cooed. "Come here. I have a treat for you."

Minx ignored her owner and promptly jumped up into Jax's lap, growling at him with her teeth bared.

"Holy hell," Ty, the young man I thought of as a son, muttered, running a hand through his dark locks.

"You can say that again," Kennedy, his partner, added.

"Ahh, she's cute, as long as she doesn't eat his face off," Aunt Lucy said.

My father, his girlfriend Tazia, and Aunt Lucy's boyfriend, Gael, all looked on the scene with wide eyes. We'd been at the end of a family dinner when my half sister,

Charlotte, had suddenly arrived, uninvited and without warning.

"Now be nice, baby," Charlotte said in a patient tone as she eyed her pup lovingly. "We don't want to overstay our welcome in the first five minutes."

Jax glanced at me and then down at the pup, who had her paws on his chest and was acting as if she was going to rip his nose off.

"Charlotte, can you get your dog before she bites Jax," I said, moving toward them.

"Oh, she's all bark and no bite," Charlotte said, flipping her long red locks over one shoulder. "Don't worry about it."

"That's easy for you to say," Jax said, leaning back to keep clear of the small dog's muzzle. His dark eyes were weary as he watched her.

"Just put her down." Charlotte moved into the kitchen and made herself right at home as she opened the cupboard and pulled out a chocolate bar I had stashed away for emergencies. She ripped it open, took a bite, and closed her eyes in obvious pleasure as the chocolate hit her tongue.

Jax reached out to the dog still snarling on his lap, but Minx lunged for his hand, barely missing taking one of his fingers off. "Son of a bitch," he muttered, eyeing the dog warily.

"Charlotte!" I cried as I reached for Minx.

The dog squatted, and before I could rescue Jax, she peed right there in his lap.

"Fuck!" He stood abruptly just as I snatched the tiny creature into my arms.

"I'm so sorry, Jax," I said, holding the dog as she snuggled happily into my chest as if she hadn't just tried to eat my boyfriend.

He glared at Charlotte and then stalked off to my bedroom.

"Well, that was quite the entrance," my father said mildly.

The rest of my family all nodded in agreement.

"Hi, Pops," Charlotte said, all smiles, not a hint of remorse in her demeanor. "You know me. I do love to put on a show."

"Charlotte," my dad said with a nod. He had a tiny smile on his face as if he were amused. A spark of anger ignited in my gut. Shouldn't he be pissed as hell? He'd done everything for her, and the minute she turned eighteen, she'd walked out, never looking back. As far as I knew, she only called him on his birthday and Christmas. It wasn't much gratitude for the man who'd treated her as his own. Where had she been when he had a cancer scare? Or when he suffered a broken leg in that car accident and needed someone to look after him for two months while he couldn't walk?

I turned to glare at my sister. She was wearing a brilliant red silk blouse that showed off her generous cleavage and a pair of painted-on jeans with the cutest red and black Mary Jane heels. "What are you doing here, Charlotte?"

She lifted her head and met my gaze. Disappointment flashed in her eyes before she straightened her shoulders and asked, "Do I need a reason to visit my only sister?"

"No, but since it's been quite some time, I'd have thought

you might call first," I said, trying to sound diplomatic. It had been ten years since I'd heard from Charlotte. I wasn't even sure how she knew where I lived now, though it was likely Dad had told her the last time they'd talked.

"It's been too long, don't you think? I was in the area and just decided to surprise you." She held out her arms, taking Minx, who was now squirming to break free of my hold. "But if it's a problem, Minx and I can find a hotel room." She frowned. "Do you know any pet friendly hotels in this town?"

I closed my eyes, trying to tame my frustration with her.

"Marion wouldn't send you to a hotel," my dad said, giving me a look that conveyed everything I needed to know. If I sent her away, he was going to have words with me.

If I was an evil child, I'd suggest she go to his house. Except he lived with my aunt Lucy, and subjecting my favorite aunt to my sister's whirlwind of chaos wasn't something I'd do.

"Of course not," I said. "The guest room is free."

Charlotte grinned at me. "Minx and I are grateful."

"You should be," I muttered to myself.

"What was that?" Charlotte narrowed her eyes, clearly having heard what I'd said.

"I said, does Minx want a cookie?" I pulled open a drawer where I kept treats for Ty and Kennedy's dog, Paris Francine, and waved the bag in her direction.

"Oh, no thank you. Minx has a delicate stomach. She only eats all organic, homemade treats that I get at the barkery."

4

I held back a snort. If they were sold at a barkery, then by definition, those treats weren't homemade. Minx whimpered as I put the bag back in the drawer. "Sorry, baby," I said to the pup. "I tried."

Charlotte let out an exaggerated sigh. "Now she's going to pout all night unless I give her one."

"So, give her one?" Ty said as he and Kennedy stood and started making their way toward me.

"She has to wait until tomorrow. We don't want to ruin her figure, now do we, Minx?" Charlotte held her dog up and made smooching noises at her.

I did my best to contain my eyeroll.

Ty had no such reservations and was clearly holding back a chuckle when he gave me a kiss on the cheek and told me that he and Kennedy were headed out to the studio apartment for the evening. After Kennedy gave me a hug, the two quickly disappeared out the front door. Aunt Lucy and Gael followed.

As Lucy gave me a hug goodbye, she whispered, "Call me later to fill me in on the drama."

I promised her a full report, and once they were gone, that left me, Charlotte, Dad, and Tazia. Jax still hadn't reappeared from my bedroom.

"Charlotte," Dad said, using his Dad tone. The one that as a child had always made me straighten up and step back into line. "What aren't you telling us?"

She gave him a look that screamed, *who, me?*

He raised one eyebrow. It would've been enough to make me spill all my secrets. But this was Charlotte. Even as a teenager, she'd never squirmed under his watchful eye, though he did seem to know how to get her to talk. And even after all this time, he still had the gift. "Charlotte Ray, you're not a teenager anymore. Wouldn't it just be simpler and easier to be straight with us? You came to Premonition Pointe and to your sister's house for a reason, right?"

Charlotte's cheeks turned pink as she averted her gaze. "I... um, well, it appears I need some help."

"With what?" I asked, narrowing my eyes at her.

"That curse I accidentally unleashed on the men down at Hallucinations." She bit her bottom lip as she grimaced, trying, and failing, to seem innocent.

I let out an exaggerated sigh and took a seat at the table, pressing my fingertips to my temples to try to mitigate the headache that was forming. "Why were you cursing anyone, let alone a bar full of men?"

"I didn't *mean* to curse them," she said, flopping down beside me. "I was trying to cast a love spell on one man in particular and then..." Her lips turned down into the pout she'd perfected as a teenager. The one that always got her out of trouble with everyone, including my father. Well, everyone except me. I saw it for what it was.

Charlotte had always used her charm and good looks to get herself out of a bind. And more often than not, I'd been the one left to pick up the pieces behind her. It was after I'd stopped putting her life together for her that she'd pulled away from us.

"A love spell? Really?" I said. "You know those never work the way you want them to."

Dad frowned, showing his disapproval, but he didn't say

anything as Charlotte raised her hands, palms up, as if to say, *oops.*

Minx jumped out of her mother's lap and into mine. She promptly rested her head on my chest and stared up at me adoringly. My heart melted right then and there. It didn't matter that her first impression had been to have an accident on Jax. In that moment, she had me wrapped around her paw with those big eyes and her sweet expression.

"Traitor," Charlotte said under her breath as she eyed her dog.

"She's brilliant," I said, scratching her ear. The dog melted against me, and I was pretty sure I'd just made a friend for life.

"She is the sweetest," Tazia added, smiling at us. She was holding Dad's hand and watching us carefully.

"And who might you be?" Charlotte asked, her tone curious but also laced with a bit of suspicion.

"Char, this is Tazia," Dad said. "She and I are dating."

"Oh." Charlotte pursed her lips. "Really? Dating?"

"They are dating. Really," I said, letting Dad off the hook. No doubt Charlotte was wondering just how serious Dad could be, considering his past dating history. Once Mom had left us all, he'd been a serial dater, never committing to anyone, no matter how right they might be for him. After all this time, he was finally giving it a shot with Tazia.

"That's great," Charlotte said, sounding like she meant it. Then she turned to me and held her hands out. "Can I have my dog back please?"

I reluctantly handed the tiny pooch over.

"It's nice that you came to Premonition Pointe," Tazia told Charlotte. "Something tells me that you and Marion could use some time together."

I studied the woman across from me. Her auburn hair was pulled up into a messy bun, and she was wearing a peasant top with a flowy skirt. She often looked like she'd just walked off the pages of a fashion magazine from the 1970s. Tonight was no different. But what one didn't usually notice at first glance was that she was a seer of sorts. She sometimes just knew things. The fact that she thought Charlotte and I should be spending time together, made me a bit nervous.

"Tazia," I said. "What's that mean exactly?"

"Yeah, I'd like to know, too," Charlotte added with a small frown.

Dad leaned across the table and said, "Tazia is a bit clairvoyant. When she talks, it's good to listen."

Charlotte looked at Tazia with renewed interest. "Yes, Tazia, tell us what you meant when you said Marion and I should spend time together."

She smirked at us. "That's not for me to say, but I will add that it looks like the two of you are in for a wild ride. I can't wait to see this."

"We always are," I said, not bothering to keep the exasperation out of my tone.

Charlotte scoffed. "Please. You act like it's always my fault that things don't go as planned."

"Isn't it?" I raised my eyebrows and stared at her pointedly.

"Hell no." She crossed her arms over her chest. "What

about that time we took that trip just before my eighteenth birthday? We ended up stranded outside of Las Vegas with a bad alternator because you told the mechanic that he and his girlfriend wouldn't last three weeks. And if that wasn't bad enough, you went on to suggest he should be dating one of his coworkers."

"Hey, that was all true," I insisted, though she had a point. I'd learned to keep my mouth shut after that. It wasn't my place to blow up relationships just because I could see if people were compatible or not.

"His coworker was a guy. Neither of them were ready to open that closet door," she said, shaking her head.

"Fine," I conceded. "You're right. I should have kept all that to myself." No one had asked my opinion. "Though I'll have you know that I did hear from them a few years later, and that guy and his coworker did finally get together. It took them a few years, but in the end it worked out."

"Sure it did. Marion always knows best," she said under her breath.

I ignored the dig. Charlotte saw me as the bossy big sister, and I saw her as the flighty, irresponsible little sister. It wasn't like either dynamic would change any time soon. After a few seconds, I looked over at her. "Tell me about this curse. What happened, exactly?"

Charlotte stared down at her dog and concentrated on petting her. The fact that she was averting my gaze was very telling. She wasn't one for contrition unless she'd done something serious.

"Char?" my dad said. "Tell us everything."

Charlotte closed her eyes for a long beat. When she

opened them, she had a determined expression on her face. "I've been seeing someone casually for about a month, and I like him a lot, but he's been really hard to read. You know, the type that takes you out, acts interested, but then goes radio silent for days on end. So I figured I'd hit him with a temporary love spell, just to speed things along a bit."

"You've been here for a month, and you just now stopped by?" I asked, more annoyed by that than the alleged curse.

"No." She scowled. "Why do you always think the worst of me?" Shaking her head, she added, "Never mind. I met him in Portland. He just moved down here, and I figured I'd come visit him and you. I got in yesterday."

I wasn't sure I believed her, but that was plausible. Unless the guy she'd been seeing cut her off after he realized he'd been cursed.

"Did the love spell work?" Tazia asked, though I could tell by her expression that she already knew the answer.

Charlotte shook her head.

"You said it was a curse," I reminded her. "How is that possible if you just cast a love spell?"

"I have no idea." She blew out a frustrated breath. "One minute I was leaning in for a kiss, and the next, Eli broke out in the worst case of acne I've ever seen. I mean, we're talking worse than a teenager with raging hormones." She visibly shuddered.

"Acne fades," I said, trying to be diplomatic.

"I hope so, because it wasn't just Eli. I gave it to every man in the bar. But that's not the worst part." Charlotte covered her face with both hands as she shook her head.

I shared a concerned look with my father. Neither of us had ever seen her like this. When she messed up as a teenager, she just shrugged it off without a care in the world. This time, though, she seemed worried. "Dare I ask, what's the worst part?"

She dropped her hands. "I broke them. All of them."

When she didn't elaborate, I said, "Charlotte, just spit it out. What happened?"

"They all got up and left. Every single one of them. The ones on dates, the ones there to hookup, and even the one who'd just asked his girlfriend to marry him. One by one, each of them left without looking back."

CHAPTER 2

"That sounds more like an anti-love spell," Iris said, wrapping her arms around her torso, trying to stave off the morning chill in the air.

"Take this," I said, offering her a spare blanket I'd brought out just for her. It was just after sunrise, and even though it was late April, the mornings were still cool near the ocean. We were sitting on my front porch because I'd wanted to talk to Iris privately about Charlotte's curse. I needed to understand just how bad it might be before we told my sister anything.

After Charlotte confessed her blunder the night before, I'd set her up in the guest room and told her we'd deal with it in the morning. My dad had said goodnight and promised to get together for lunch sometime soon. I still wasn't sure how I felt about his reaction to Charlotte just breezing back into our lives after having been gone for ten years. He seemed... pleased to see her. Meanwhile, I was suspicious.

And if I was honest, a little bitter. He'd raised her since she was eight as if she were his own. Then she'd left without even a note, leaving me to pick up the pieces.

"Thanks." Iris draped the blanket over her and then picked up the cup of coffee sitting on the side table. "I am more than ready for the summer weather to make a showing."

"Same." I took a sip from my own mug and was just about to ask what we could do about the curse when the front door suddenly swung open and Jax stumbled out.

"Let go, you little monster!" he ordered, shaking his right leg.

Minx had her teeth planted in the hem of his jeans and was shaking her head while growling as if she were going to chew his ankle off.

"Minx!" I called, standing and reaching for the little dog. But she darted to the right, moving so she was just out of my reach.

Riiiip.

The Chihuahua tore a large hole in Jax's pant leg, shaking her head violently as if that wasn't nearly enough to satisfy her.

"Son of a mother-effing shit," Jax spit out, shaking his leg to try to safely dislodge the dog. "If you break the skin, we're gonna have some serious words," he told her.

I bit back a laugh. The situation wasn't funny, but the fact that he was doing his best not to lose his temper or do anything that might hurt Minx made my heart swell with love for the man. He had every right to be beyond pissed that my sister's dog seemed to want to eat him alive, but Jax was being as patient with the tiny creature as anyone could expect.

"That's enough, Minx!" I called out in my no-nonsense voice. The dog froze and turned her big eyes up at him. "Let go. Now."

She promptly let go of Jax's torn pant leg and tucked her tail down between her legs.

"Come here, baby," I said softly.

The chihuahua hurried over to me and practically jumped into my arms. "It's not nice to attack people, Minx. Jax is a good guy. He's not going to hurt anyone. You don't need to take a foot off."

She stuffed her little face between my arm and my torso, effectively hiding from her small audience.

I glanced up at Jax, who was busy checking out his torn jeans. "Did she break the skin?"

Jax shook his head and grimaced as he checked out the damage to his jeans. "She only managed to mangle my last clean pair of pants."

"Sorry." I gave him a small sympathetic smile. "I'd offer to mend them, but it looks like that hem is beyond repair." Minx had shredded the part she'd managed to tear from his pantleg. "I could buy you a new pair."

He glanced up and frowned. "Why would you buy them? Minx isn't your dog."

"No, but Charlotte is my sister, and I can't imagine that she'll ever offer up reimbursement."

He shook his head. "Don't worry about it. It's not your fault."

I glanced back at the front door. "What happened here? Why didn't Charlotte stop Minx from attacking you?"

"Your sister went to shower and left Minx in the kitchen with a bowl of water and some food. She was perfectly occupied until she heard me come into the kitchen for coffee. But then it was like something out of a *Gremlins* movie. Like she'd eaten and lost her mind. She saw me, bared her teeth, and launched herself in my direction, snarly and ready to draw blood."

"Ready to draw blood?" Iris asked, sounding amused. "The poor dog barely even has teeth."

Jax narrowed his eyes at her. "Just wait until she's trying to eat your face off, then we'll see how harmless you think her teeth are."

Iris held her hands up in a surrender motion. "Sorry. I know she was attacking your leg. I saw it with my own two eyes. It's just hard to imagine her going from this"—she waved a hand at me and Minx, who'd promptly fallen asleep in my arms—"to a snarling hell beast. She just seems so sweet."

"*Seems* is the operative word here," Jax said dryly.

I reached out and squeezed his hand. "I'm sorry. I'm sure she'll get used to you."

He gave me a skeptical look but returned my squeeze and said, "I'm going to head into town and get my coffee there before I take care of a few errands. I'll call you later, all right?"

"Sounds good. And sorry about the coffee deprivation," I said, wondering if I'd see him that night. Usually we had dinner together and Jax stayed over. But after the reception he'd gotten from Minx and the fact that my sister was now staying at my house, I wouldn't be surprised if he kept his distance. I would.

"Me, too." He gave me a tiny smile as he lifted my hand and gave it a kiss. No doubt, he didn't want to lean over the hellhound to kiss me on the lips and risk getting his throat ripped out if she noticed him.

"Looks like Minx has a problem with men," Iris said.

"Like most women we know who've been mistreated?" I joked.

Iris chuckled. "It's true. Trust is a tough one when a girl has been wronged."

"It'll be okay, Minx," I said, scratching her ear as I sat back down. "Jax is one of the good ones."

Minx let out a little growl but then snuggled into my blanket, content to be in my lap.

I let out a small sigh and looked over at Iris. "She's not going to warm up to him, is she?"

"Doesn't look like it'll be anytime soon," Iris agreed. "Now, tell me about this curse your sister unleashed on the unsuspecting men of Premonition Pointe."

I quickly filled her in on how Charlotte's love spell had backfired. "Now we have an undisclosed number of men here in Premonition Pointe who've been cursed."

Iris's lips twitched with amusement as she quickly pressed her hand to her mouth. "Oh, Marion. I'm sorry. I know it isn't funny, but the idea of the men down at Hallucinations suddenly being cock-blocked by a backfired spell is just too much."

"Well, when you put it that way..." I shook my head,

DEANNA CHASE

chuckling with her. Then I quickly sobered. "But what do we do about it?"

She shrugged one shoulder. "Nothing. The curse should just wear off on its own. Did we ever tell you about the time Grace accidentally cursed her ex-husband with erectile dysfunction?"

My eyes widened. "She did? How did she accidentally do that?"

"She was angry and was thinking about it. Sometimes strong emotions can make things happen even if you aren't trying to cast a spell. Served him right, the two-timing bastard. But alas, those kinds of spells fade with a little bit of time. I'm sure everyone will be back to normal shortly."

I choked out a laugh. "Grace is now my hero." I pursed my lips as I considered what Iris had said. "If he was her ex, then how did she find out about his... ah, problem?"

"His new girlfriend blurted it out." Iris shook with laughter. "That was after she left him of course. I hear he's still single. Turns out most women in a town as small as Premonition Pointe aren't too excited to date a cheater."

"No, I'd guess not." Anyone who'd cheat on the lovely Grace Valentine deserved whatever he got in the karma department.

Iris patted my leg and stood. "Don't worry about your sister's little mishap. I'm sure everyone will be back to normal in a few days." She smirked. "I'm sure at least a few of them could use the ego check anyway."

I chuckled. "That's cold, Iris."

She shrugged. "I'm just speaking the truth." Iris waved as she started walking to her car. "See you at the office later."

18

I returned the wave and took a long sip of my coffee, wondering how long I could stay on the porch before Charlotte came looking for me.

"Marion!" my sister cried from inside the house, her voice full of panic. "Where is she? Minx? Where are you, sweetie?"

"We're out here," I called back, rising from my chair and heading for the door.

A loud crash came from inside the house, making me wince.

"Everything okay in here?" I asked, holding Minx to my chest as we peered inside.

"Your plant got in the way," Charlotte said angrily as she held her hands out for her dog. "Come to mama, baby."

Minx curled tighter to my chest, her little claws digging into my arm. "You might want to calm down a bit, Char. Minx seems a little tense."

"She's not tense. She's upset because she didn't know where I was." Charlotte took Minx out of my arms and held her up so that she could blow kisses at her.

Minx turned her face away and looked at me.

I swallowed a grimace. This was not going to go well. If Charlotte's dog appeared to be happier with me than with her, my sister was going to lose her shit.

"Seriously? After all I've done for you?" Charlotte scoffed. "Now you're just gonna turn your back on me for someone you've never even met before?"

I gave them a wide berth and headed into my kitchen where I found a half-eaten bowl of kibble on the floor, a bag of unfamiliar coffee, and coffee grinds coating the counter.

Son of a... *Ugh.* I grabbed a fresh dishcloth and went to work on cleaning my space. Once I had the counters sparkling, I glanced over at Charlotte. "Will Minx finish this, or can we put it up?"

She waved an unconcerned hand. "Just leave it. She takes her time digesting. She'll eat when she's ready."

I ground my teeth, knowing that if Ty or Kennedy brought Paris Francine, their sweet Yorkie, into the house, she'd make a beeline for it. Hopefully I'd remember to warn them if they showed up. They were living in the apartment above the garage, but they regularly visited the house.

"I'm starving," Charlotte said, staring into my refrigerator. "You don't have anything but cheese and lettuce in here."

"That's just not true," I insisted. "There are all kinds of veggies in the crisper, yogurt, leftover lasagna, and some bacon."

"The veggies are decomposing, your yogurt is expired, and the bacon looks like a science experiment. None of that is giving me confidence that the lasagna is safe to eat. Not that I want that for breakfast anyway."

"Oh, come on, it's not that bad." I pulled the fridge door open and peered in. A moment later, I sighed heavily and started throwing the expired things out. "So I needed to clean out my fridge. Don't judge. Here." I handed her the freshly purchased yogurt. "I just got this a few days ago. And the lasagna is from last night."

Charlotte let out a self-deprecating laugh. "Who's judging? I don't even have a fridge, let alone rotting lettuce.

But I'm not in the mood for yogurt. Is there a good breakfast place around here?"

"No fridge? Don't you have a place up in Portland?" I asked. Hadn't she mentioned that's where she'd been before coming to see the boyfriend she'd cursed?

"No. My lease was up. Since you and Dad and the guy I'd been casually dating was here, I figured I'd relocate."

Perfect timing, Char, I thought with a heavy dose of sarcasm, but I kept it to myself.

I finished clearing out the fridge, and the tomatoes that had gotten far too soft landed with a quiet thud in my garbage can. While I quickly washed my hands, I said, "There are crepes waiting for us at the Bird's Eye Café. Be ready in five minutes."

My sister's eyes lit up. "I'll be ready in two."

CHAPTER 3

"*I* can't believe you ordered three kinds," I said, eyeing all the plates in front of Charlotte.

"Choosing was just too hard." She pointed at her blueberry crepes. "These are delicious. If you don't order some immediately, I'm going to assume you've suffered a head injury in the not so distant past."

"I'm happy with my cinnamon custard for today, but I'll try the blueberry next time." I shoved another bite of yummy goodness into my mouth.

"Brain injury," Charlotte muttered, shaking her head. "It's such a shame."

I rolled my eyes but couldn't suppress a small laugh. She was the same old Charlotte, always giving everyone shit.

"Why are you looking at me like that?" she asked, frowning as she studied me.

"Like what?" I put my fork down and reached for my mocha latte.

"Like you're amused. That's not normal. You never used to like it when I poked at you."

This time my chuckle was louder. "Maybe I'm just mellower now. Or you're funnier? Maybe both. Now eat. This breakfast is delicious."

She took a bite and then put her fork down, looking serious. "You know what I never understood?"

I paused before taking another bite. "What's that?"

"I never used to understand why my presence bothered you so much. No matter what I did, I always seemed to annoy you. Was it because I just existed? I could understand that, you know. It's not normal for your mother to leave your father, have another kid, come running back and then leave again, this time for good. But I didn't have any control over that, so I'd always hoped you'd stop blaming me." She dropped her gaze to her plate and pushed the half-eaten crepe around.

"Charlotte, that's not—" I started.

"Stop." She held up her hand. "Please don't try to tell me that was all in my head. I know it wasn't. It's why I left."

That left me speechless. She'd left because of me? "Damn, Char. I'm sorry," I said, meaning it. "I never meant to make you feel that way. I honestly never blamed you." That was the truth, too. I hadn't. Though I could see now why she thought so.

"That's not how it seemed to me," she said, this time staring me in the eye.

I took a deep breath. "I can see that. Back then..." I shook my head. "When you came to live with Dad, I was still in my twenties, and I hadn't figured my life out yet. Dad was a mess. I'm not sure you knew that back then, but he was. He probably hid it from you, but not from me. So I was dealing with issues of Mom leaving, Dad falling apart, and me trying to help him raise a sister I'd just found out I had. To say I didn't handle it that well would be an understatement. I'm sorry I made you feel anything less than wanted. But know this, I never wanted you to leave, and it hurt when you did."

It was her turn to blow out a long breath. "I needed to figure some stuff out on my own."

"Sure." I nodded. "Understandable. Neither one of us had the most stable upbringing. And while Dad is great, Mom really did a number on both of us."

"You can say that again," she muttered.

I gave her a sympathetic smile. "I'm glad you're back though."

"You are?" There was a heavy dose of skepticism in her tone.

Laughing, I nodded. "I'm still adjusting, but I am glad to see you."

"Does that mean I can stay in your guest room until I find a job and get settled?"

I sputtered on my coffee, making her laugh. "You want to keep staying at my house?"

"Where else? Aunt Lucy's? You're not going to subject me to having to listen to geriatric sex noises, are you? Now that she and Pops are coupled up—"

I held my hand up, stopping her. "Stop. That is not a visual I need. You can stay."

She grinned. "Great. I'm glad we got that settled."

It was on the tip of my tongue to tell her we still needed to work out something about Minx trying to eat Jax when I was interrupted by another patron.

"Excuse me. Do you mind if we steal a couple of these chairs?" a sleek, dark-haired woman in stylish knee-high boots, jeans, and an oversized sweater asked. Before I could even answer, she had one of the chairs already at the next table and was picking up the next one.

I raised an eyebrow. "Would if matter if I said no?"

The woman let out a loud chuckle as if I'd just said something witty instead of snarking at her. Albeit, admittedly for no good reason. No one was going to be joining us. However, she did pause before placing the second chair at her table. "Sorry. I'm just excited for my girls' brunch. I can find other chairs if it's a problem."

Charlotte waived a hand. "Oh no. We're not using them. Please, take them. And I apologize for my sister. I think she didn't quite get enough rest last night. Her hot boyfriend made sure of that."

"Charlotte!" I admonished, irritated that heat was crawling up my neck and toward my cheeks. Had my sister heard me and Jax the night before, or was she just being salacious to embarrass me? I could only hope the latter was the case.

"Good for you." The woman winked at me and then took a seat with her party.

"It's not my fault you need to soundproof your walls." Charlotte took a sip of her coffee and smirked at me.

I was about to tell her that if we bothered her, she could pay for the soundproofing herself, when a blond-haired woman next to us blurted, "My husband thinks he's been cursed."

Both Charlotte and I turned our attention to the women.

"Seriously? What's the curse? One that makes him incapable of loading the dishwasher or taking the garbage out?" Her friend with the sleek dark locks chuckled. "Because that would explain a lot when it comes to my husband."

The other two women nodded in agreement.

"No, no," the blonde said, shaking her head. "It's not that. In fact, I have to give him credit. Ever since I went on a household-chores strike last fall, he's been much better about that. This is... well, he came down with a serious case of acne, which is not at all normal and he has," she lowered her voice, "a bedroom issue."

"You mean he's blaming his erectile dysfunction on a curse?" the petite one with black pigtails and combat boots said with a loud laugh. "That's a new one. What's the cure? A trip to the strip club?"

"No." The blonde waved her hands as if to wipe away their comments. "He was at Hallucinations last night, sexting me—"

"Did he send you dick pics?" one of them asked.

The blonde's cheeks turned bright red as she nodded. "He went into the restroom and took a couple of shots for me and was just about to leave when he said something happened. The lights flickered, and he felt some weird sensation before all the desire was zapped out of him. He hurried home, and no amount of effort could bring back that erection. And trust me, I gave it my all. There was just no blowing it back to life."

Charlotte sucked in a sharp breath.

"Maybe he has whiskey dick," one of them said, giving her a sympathetic smile. "It happens.

It was clear the blonde's friends weren't taking this seriously. But after Charlotte's announcement the night before, I was more inclined to believe that he had indeed been cursed with erectile dysfunction. Or at least with the anti-love spell that caused his condition. I wanted to lean over and assure the woman that the spell would wear off… eventually. That's what Iris had said, anyway. But then I'd have to admit I was eavesdropping, and the truth was, I wasn't completely sure the curse would wear off. Or if it did, when that might be. It was better to keep my thoughts to myself. I didn't want to make things worse for anyone, including Charlotte, who was the one responsible for the mayhem unleashed on the men at Hallucinations the night before.

We both finished our breakfasts with minimal chitchat. When we were done, I paid the bill and the two of us walked out onto Main Street. I started to head for the car, but Charlotte grabbed my arm and said, "I'm worried."

"About?" I asked, surprised she was confiding in me. When she was younger, Charlotte took everything in stride and acted like no matter what happened, everything would work out in her favor. But today, there were worry lines etched around her eyes and her forehead was pinched.

"This isn't the first time this has happened."

I stopped mid-step and stared at my sister. "What do you mean, exactly?"

She cleared her throat and stared out toward the water. "It's not the first time I've cast a spell and had it go haywire."

"It's not?" I studied her, taking in her hunched shoulders and the worry in her green eyes. "What happened before?"

She swallowed. Hard. "I, um, did a simple compulsion spell, and—"

"Charlotte!" Compulsion spells forced people to do things against their will. They were highly illegal and completely unethical. "What the hell were you thinking?" Even with everything I knew about my sister, I never thought she'd resort to forcing anyone to do something against their will.

"It was just a tiny spell to get my boyfriend to remember my birthday. Geez! It wasn't like I was compelling him to empty his bank account or buy me a fancy diamond. I just wanted him to remember."

The righteous indignation that had filled my chest started to fade. The spell was still unethical and a minor crime, but it wasn't like witches all over the country didn't use it for the exact same purpose. Usually a spell like that was harmless. I narrowed my eyes at her. "What happened after you compelled him?"

She glanced away and muttered, "He started doing everything I said."

I raised one eyebrow. "Like?"

"Like everything, Marion. As soon as I asked for the remote, he jumped up, found it, and brought it to me. If I said I was hungry, he'd hurry into the kitchen and start making me something. If I mentioned I had a craving for donuts, he'd immediately jump in the car and go get my favorites. If I told him to stop talking, he stayed mute for hours until I told him he could talk again. He did my bidding, and even when I ordered him to stop, he didn't. He couldn't."

A pit formed in my stomach. "Tell me you figured out how to neutralize the compulsion spell."

She slowly shook her head as tears glistened in her eyes. "I tried. Multiple times. But nothing ever worked. Eventually, I told him it was over and left."

"Charlotte," I whispered, my tone full of compassion. "Do you know how he's doing now?"

She nodded as a single tear rolled down her cheek. "He's engaged to a very pretty woman with two shih tzus. I made a point of checking to make sure he's not affected by the compulsion spell. It's only a problem if I'm the one telling him what to do."

My heart ached for her. It was clear she'd really cared about this man and had let him go for his own good. "I'm so sorry, Char." I reached out and squeezed her hand. "That's terrible."

Her voice trembled as she met my eyes and said, "Marion, I think I'm broken."

This was a side of my sister I'd never seen before. As a surly teenager, frightened wasn't an emotion she'd shown anyone. Ever.

Her eyes turned pleading as she asked, "Can you help me?"

There was no hesitation. It didn't matter that we'd spent

ten years not talking. Charlotte was my sister. And no matter what, I loved her. Not to mention, I couldn't just sit around and do nothing about the curse she'd unleashed on the innocent men of Premonition Pointe. "I'll do whatever I can."

CHAPTER 4

"*M*arion!" Celia, my resident ghost, called the moment she popped into my office. "You will never believe what I heard down at *Abs, Buns, and Guns.*"

"Half the men in Premonition Pointe have erectile dysfunction?" I asked as I opened an email from a prospective client.

"No, but tell me more about that." She sat on the edge of my desk and crossed her arms over her chest, interest dancing in her big blue Kewpie doll eyes.

"Give me just a minute." I gave my full attention to my inbox and tapped out a response to the man who was looking for a same-sex partner who was career-driven and also liked to travel. Most of my client base in Premonition Pointe had been people looking for partners of the opposite sex, so I was happy to be expanding my client base to the LGBTQ community.

"I'm here," Iris said, closing the door behind her. "Hello,

Celia." She nodded at the ghost and placed her shoulder bag on the desk she used when she was working in the office. Iris was my business manager, but since the agency was up and running full speed, she'd cut down on the time she spent in the office so she could work with other business owners who needed a little help.

"Thank the goddess." I clicked out of my email and smiled at her. "Celia has something to tell us."

"Do I ever," Celia said. "The women of this town are about to get very cranky when they find out that the filming for *The Witch Island Bride* has been postponed indefinitely. And if what Marion said about half the town having ED is true, then this town is desperately gonna need a sex toy shop. I saw there's a storefront for rent a few doors down. That would be the perfect location."

Both Iris and I turned to give her our full attention.

"Say that again," Iris said.

Celia rolled her eyes. "Flaccid junk. Limp pickles. Defective love sticks. This town is in dire need of a sex toy shop. The amount of penis pumps they'd unload could probably cover startup costs."

"Celia," Iris said, exasperation in her tone. "I was talking about the postponement of the filming for *The Witch Island Bride*. What happened?"

"Oh. That." The ghost waved an unconcerned hand. "It's been postponed because Damon Grant broke his ankle last night. Can't make a movie when the hero is out of commission, can they? There's even talk about scrapping it until next year so they can focus on making the next movie in the pipeline. Time is money and all that."

34

"We need to call Joy and Carly," Iris said, already picking up her phone.

"I'll call Carly," I said.

She nodded, her phone already to her ear.

I quickly scrolled until I found Carly's number. It immediately went to voice mail. I left her a message, offering support and a girls' night if she needed it. The movie was supposed to feature Carly Preston and Joy Lancing as undercover witches who protect their small island off the coast of California from evil forces. Joy's character was scripted to get married, but her heartthrob fiancé has no idea she's a witch. It was a romantic suspense with comedic elements that was supposed to be a major release for the spring blockbuster season next year. This was a devastating blow for both our friends, but especially for Joy, whose career was just taking off.

"Joy didn't answer either," Iris said, slumping in her chair. "This is terrible." She glanced at Celia. "How did Damon break his ankle?"

The ghost snorted. "The dumb idiot got drunk and slipped as he was leaving Hallucinations last night."

I choked on my own spit. "Hallucinations? Are you sure?"

She shrugged one shoulder. "That's what I heard from multiple people. Why?"

"Son of a... dammit. I'd bet my last dollar it wasn't because he was drunk."

"You think some eager barfly got overzealous and rushed him?" Celia asked, a glint in her eye. "I wouldn't exactly blame her. That man is hot with a capital H."

"No." I grimaced as I added, "I think he was cursed. By my sister."

Iris stiffened. "Oh, no. You're probably right."

"I didn't know you have a sister!" Celia jumped up and started to pace. "And you think she cursed the hottest man to hit the airwaves since David Hasselhoff?"

"Did you really just say David Hasselhoff?" I asked, choking back a laugh. Was she serious? "How do you even know who he is?"

"Please." She flipped her long blond hair over her shoulder. "*Baywatch* and *Knight Rider* are the two best shows ever made."

"I think that's up for serious debate," I said. "Still, both of those shows were way before your time. How do you even know about them?"

Her grin softened to a nostalgic smile. "My mama was a fan."

Iris nodded. "Mine, too."

I shook my head. "Anyway, yes. I'm pretty sure my sister is ground zero for his accident. She and I haven't been particularly close for the past several years, but she came to town and tried to cast a love spell. Unfortunately, it backfired and appeared to curse all the men in the bar. I just hope no one else was seriously injured by her mistake."

"What kind of spell was she casting?" Celia asked, her tone curious.

"A love spell, but it backfired and turned into a curse." I met Iris's gaze. "I know you said the curse was likely to wear off, but I learned today that this isn't the first time it's happened. And last time, the spell didn't fade."

Iris's eyes widened. "Really? What happened?"

I filled her and Celia in on Charlotte's ex-boyfriend and then slumped in my chair. "I think she needs a healer or a magical psychologist or something so this doesn't happen again."

"She needs to stop casting spells immediately," Iris said, already picking up the phone.

"I know. I told her that. But what if she accidentally casts one like Grace did a while back?"

"I can keep an eye on her," Celia volunteered.

"How would that stop her from accidentally cursing someone?" I asked, frowning at the ghost.

"I don't know." She shrugged. "Don't you need intel or something? Like why her spells are turning into curses? Maybe I'll see something she's not telling you. You and your sister aren't exactly on the best of terms, right?"

"What makes you think that?" I crossed my arms over my chest as I studied her.

"I've been hanging around you for quite a while now, Marion. You talk to your aunt, your dad, your son, and that bestie of yours down in LA on a regular basis. You are the type of person who keeps in touch with your loved ones even if you're the one who has to do all the calling. I don't think for one minute you wouldn't be chatting her up on the regular if there wasn't something coming between the two of you."

Damn. My ghost seemed to know me better than most of my friends. Celia was outrageous on a regular basis, but this just proved that she was more insightful and deeper than I usually gave her credit for.

"Yeah. You're right, Celia. But hopefully, now that she's in town, we can move past all of our issues. And I don't think having my ghostly employee spying on her is the best way to go about mending things between us. She isn't interested in cursing anyone; that much I know. So she won't be doing anything on purpose. I think the best plan of action is for her to work with the coven to hone her magic skills so that no more accidents happen."

Celia gave me a skeptical look. "You're really turning me down? You already know I'm great at shadowing people."

That was true. She'd done it for me when I needed to keep an eye on Kennedy a few weeks ago and when we'd thought Lennon Love was in danger. When it came to investigative monitoring, she really was my go-to person… err, ghost. "Your skills aren't in question," I said with a definitive nod. "I just don't think following her is the right move. If that changes, I'll be sure to let you know."

She pursed her lips, looking unconvinced, but then raised her hands, palms up. "If you say so, boss. I'll leave your little sis alone. If you don't need me to do that, what else would you like me to work on?"

I sat back in my chair and tapped a key on my computer. "You can help by keeping an eye out for Charlotte's victims from Hallucinations. I want to know if their curses are fading, staying the same, or getting worse."

She raised an eyebrow. "How am I supposed to find these victims?"

"Do what you do best. Spy on the people of Premonition Pointe."

"Including the hottie from *The Witch Island Bride?*" she asked hopefully.

"Yes. Including Damon Grant."

She pumped a fist into the air. "Yes! This job rocks."

Celia vanished from the office with a loud pop, leaving silence in her wake.

Iris cleared her throat. "Do you think that was a good idea?"

I smirked. "Probably not, but she's harmless... mostly."

CHAPTER 5

I stood in my kitchen, staring at my phone, wondering what just happened.

The front door swung open and Minx went off, barking as if she was going to rip someone's throat out.

"Whoa, girl." Kennedy's soothing voice floated into the kitchen from the other room. "Paris Francine just wants to say hi. No need to try to take an ear off."

I peeked around the corner, finding Kennedy crouched down and petting Minx as he kept a protective hand on his Yorkie. The fact that she was letting him meant she didn't hate all men. So far it was only Jax she wanted to shred to pieces.

"That's it, Minx. Paris is safe. She just wants to play." He gently lifted his hands off the two dogs, allowing them to sniff each other. It only took a few moments before Minx started to wag her tail vigorously, and then the two pups took off through the house, roughhousing and having the time of their lives.

"Thanks for bringing Paris over," I said, leaning against the doorframe. "Minx has chewed a hole in every single sock she's gotten her little jaws on. Despite the three dozen toys Charlotte has strewn around the house for her, she apparently only wants to make sure I have frozen toes for next winter."

Kennedy laughed. "No problem. Paris needs the play time, too." He glanced at the two pups who were rolling around and half-heartedly trying to eat each other's faces off. "The sock thing means she likes you."

"I don't think so," I said. "She never eats Charlotte's socks."

"Exactly." He gave me a knowing look before both of us snickered.

"You're terrible," I said, grinning at him as we moved into the kitchen. I immediately started making him a cup of afternoon coffee while he fished the shortbread out of the cupboard.

"It's what makes me interesting."

"I'd argue it's what makes you fun." Once we had our coffees in hand and the cookies on a serving plate, we settled at the kitchen table. I turned to him with what I hoped was an apologetic expression. "My dad just called and summoned us to a family dinner. He's requested that you and Ty meet us at Blueberries at six."

His eyebrows shot up. Then he shook his head. "Uh, that might be an issue."

"Please don't tell me you guys have plans tonight," I

begged. "If you don't come, it's just going to be me, Charlotte, Dad, and Tazia. I could use a buffer." Even though Charlotte and I had talked things out this morning and things were fine between us, I was still feeling a little raw about... everything.

"I'm sorry." He reached over and patted my shoulder. "But Skyler invited us over for dinner, and since he's my boss..."

"Dammit," I muttered and felt a throb start at my temple.

"I guess I could ask him to reschedule?" Kennedy said, sounding anything but pleased by the idea.

"No, no." I waved a hand. "Don't you dare do any such thing. It's much more important that you schmooze with your boss instead of providing me cover at my dad's last-minute summons."

"I'm sure it won't be that bad," Kennedy said, but his expression clearly indicated he didn't believe a word he said.

I let out a humorless laugh. "Right. Famous last words."

"COME ON, CHAR. WE'RE LATE," I said, tapping my foot while my sister took forever to exit the car. "Dad doesn't care if you have a fresh coat of lipstick."

Charlotte let out an exaggerated sigh as her stylish purple Mary Janes finally hit the asphalt. "We're only five minutes late. Calm down. It's not like he's going to get up and leave if we aren't there right on the dot."

"No, but it's rude to keep people waiting." I wasn't sure

why I was picking a fight with her. She was right. We weren't unreasonably late. If Dad and Tazia were already inside, they'd just get a table and order drinks.

"You're too wound up," Charlotte said. "You'd think with all the mattress gymnastics you've been doing with that boyfriend of yours, you'd be a lot more relaxed."

I bit back a retort. It was none of her business what Jax and I did behind closed doors. And I certainly wasn't going to confirm or deny anything. Though, she was right about that, too. We spent nearly every night together, and there was hardly a night that went by that he didn't show me exactly how much I turned him on.

The scent of fresh baked bread overwhelmed my senses the moment we stepped into Blueberries. I'd only been there a couple times before, but the farm-to-table restaurant was already one of my favorites.

Charlotte waltzed over to the table by the window and took the seat next to Dad. She leaned over and gave him a big hug. Dad's arms went around her, and a genuine smile lit up his whole face.

"Hey, kid," he said and gave her a kiss on the top of her head. "It's really good to see you again."

"Right back at ya, Pops." She held on for a beat longer than necessary, and when she pulled away, her eyes were glassy as if she'd been holding back tears.

My own eyes welled with emotion, but I forced it back. While it was good to see her connecting with him, that didn't change the fact that she'd disappeared from both our lives ten years ago. Charlotte and I hadn't exactly been close because of our age difference, but I had helped raise her and

I'd been hurt. I couldn't imagine what it must've been like for Dad. He'd given her all of himself. He'd been the father she'd needed when her own hadn't stepped up. It had nearly killed me to see her take off like she had. He hadn't deserved that. I supposed that's why I'd spent the last ten years being resentful. After our talk, though, I vowed to let that go. She'd had her reasons, and I needed to respect them.

"So," I said, diving right in. "What's the meaning of this family gathering? Do we have business to discuss or is this just a social thing?"

Tazia glanced at my dad and then back at me. There was tension in her shoulders and her expression. Uh-oh. That meant there was something he wanted to talk about. I braced myself for whatever it might be.

Dad picked up his amber-colored drink, took a sip, and then casually said, "Let's just have dinner, okay?"

"I'm all for dinner," Charlotte said enthusiastically. "This place smells delicious."

I eyed my father. On the surface, he seemed relaxed and happy to just be out with his daughters, but there was a slight stiffness to his jaw and his smile seemed a little forced. What was Memphis Matched up to? It seemed obvious to me that this meeting wasn't just about a family dinner.

It didn't look like I was going to find out anytime soon, though. As my dad asked Charlotte how long she planned to stay in town, I opened the drink menu and prayed they had something stronger than wine. I was going to need it.

"I haven't set a time limit," Charlotte said. "I've been wanting to relocate, so I thought I'd hang out and try

Premonition Pointe on for size. I always did love the beach. Minx is a fan, too."

My dad's eyes lit up. "Really? Well, that certainly would be wonderful having you near again. And I know your Aunt Lucy would love to spend more time with you, too."

"What about you, Marion?" Charlotte asked me.

I choked on the sip of water I'd just taken. "Um, what?" I sputtered through my coughing fit. My eyes started to water as Charlotte patted my back, trying to help.

"Are you okay?" she asked.

I glanced up at her and nearly jerked back when I spotted her aura. It was a fiery red, just as it had always been, but this time it had a tinge of yellow around the edges, indicating that while she was still a spitfire, there was a softening of her emotional state. As if maybe she was starting to become a little mellower with age.

"What?" Charlotte asked, pulling her hand away.

Her aura vanished.

"Holy crow," I whispered as I blinked rapidly and then reached out and touched her hand. It took a second, but her aura came roaring back. That hadn't happened earlier when I'd touched her. Why was it happening now? More importantly, why was it happening at all?

Tears stung my eyes as I turned and looked at Dad and Tazia. Their complimentary auras were back in full force, making me chuckle through a sob that had formed in my throat. I hadn't realized until that very moment just how much I'd missed my ability to see auras. A part of me had been broken, and now I felt whole. I turned back to my sister and beamed.

She pulled her hand back as if she'd been burned. "That was… surreal. Why am I seeing auras when you touch me?"

"You saw them, too?" I gasped out. That wasn't Charlotte's gift.

"Yeah. Just now, but not this morning when I touched you. Yours is really dark, like indigo, while those two over there," she said, pointing to Dad and Tazia, "are swimming in purple. It's a little nauseating to be honest."

"You saw our auras?" Dad asked me.

I nodded, blinking back the sting of tears in my eyes.

"Of course she did," Charlotte answered for me. "She's always seen them. Why is that a big deal?"

"It's a big deal because Marion was cursed not long ago and lost her aura-seeing abilities," Tazia explained. Her gaze flickered from Charlotte to me and back to Charlotte. "It looks like you might be the key to her rediscovering that ability."

"Me?" Charlotte placed her hand on her chest and looked at Tazia as if she'd lost her mind. "No way. That's impossible. I'm… Well, magic isn't exactly my strong suit."

"What do you mean, Charlotte might be the answer?" I asked Tazia. Dad's girlfriend was a seer of sorts. She sometimes just knew things. And while I'd been a little skeptical about that in the past, she'd been right often enough that I now listened when she spoke.

"You two appear to be complements to each other. I'm sensing you might have had some sort of breakthrough in your relationship today that perhaps helped foster this development," Tazia said with a knowing nod. "I think this is going to be spectacular."

"How?" I asked.

"Just wait. You'll see." She grinned at me.

Charlotte and I stared at each other. She looked perplexed, and I was certain my expression mirrored hers.

But then the waiter arrived and we all ordered dinner. For the next hour we enjoyed our meal as Tazia talked about her flowers and the small wholesale nursery she was opening. It seemed she'd already lined up some wholesale accounts.

"Are you looking for any help?" Charlotte asked. "I'm really good at sales."

Tazia bit her lower lip as she studied my sister. "I might be able to use a part-time helper, but that would be on the farm, doing manual labor."

"Oh." Charlotte looked at her nails. "That's not really what I'm looking for."

I snorted. "Charlotte doesn't really like the outdoors."

She shrugged, not denying it.

"I think Charlotte should work for you, Marion," Tazia said.

"What?" my sister and I said at the same time. That seemed like a terrible idea. We were just finding common ground after all this time. If she worked for me, that could be a recipe for disaster. If Charlotte had to take orders from me, how would we ever move past the big-sister-little-sister dynamic? But there was no way I could just dismiss the idea. Not after learning that I could see auras again when we were connected. I quickly reached over and placed my hand on her arm. Auras immediately came to life all over the restaurant.

"Marion, stop touching me," she whined like an eight-year-old who thought her sister had cooties.

"Fine." I released her arm. "But Tazia is onto something. I don't know why, but touching you makes me able to see auras again. If you came to work for me, it would make my job a hundred times easier. All I'd need you to do is be there when I'm evaluating if two people are a potential love match."

"That's all?" she asked, raising a skeptical eyebrow.

"Well, I'll probably ask you to do some admin duties. Help with planning mixers. Client interviews. You know, matchmaking stuff." It wasn't like we had mixers every day, which was where I'd previously found matches by evaluating auras.

"Admin? Like computer work?" She wrinkled her nose. "Computers give me a headache. I don't think so. Unless..." Charlotte trailed off as she eyed a model-gorgeous waiter as he walked by.

"Unless what?" I asked, narrowing my eyes at her.

She turned to me with an impish grin. "If you find me a love match, I'll come work with you."

"Wait, you want me to set you up with someone? Seriously?" I asked, not at all sure what I thought about that.

"Yes, seriously. Why? Do you not want to find me someone? Don't I deserve love, too?" she asked, indignant as she stared me down.

"Of course you do," I said automatically. "I just... Well, I'm in the business of finding people their love matches when they want to find their *forever* person. Are you sure that's what you're looking for?" Charlotte had just blown into town without a place to live or a job to see some guy she'd been casually dating, only to end up cursing him and a bunch of other men in town. Now she wanted me to help her find a boyfriend? It seemed to me that she should have more important priorities.

"Maybe I'm looking for some stability, did you ever think about that? Did you miss the part where I cast an ill-advised love spell? Why do you think I did that?" She grimaced. "Ugh, I sound pathetic." Her expression turned vulnerable as she added, "Would it be so terrible if I settled down here, near my family? I could do it alone, but I'd prefer it if I had someone by my side. Someone other than my bossy older sister who sees me as a flighty screwup."

I wanted to say that I didn't see her that way, but it would be a lie, wouldn't it? Wasn't that exactly what I'd been thinking since the moment she blew into town? Since she'd left ten years ago? That wasn't fair. Charlotte was a decade older, and although she'd gotten herself into a few messes, she'd certainly grown up quite a bit. Our conversation earlier proved that. "Okay. I'll do it. But *after* we fix your love spell curse."

"It sounds like a decent trade, Marion," Tazia said softly.

"That's because you aren't the one who has to be the matchmaker," I told Tazia, giving her an easy smile. "But I'm a pro, and I could really use Charlotte." I held my hand out to my sister. "You've got a deal."

Charlotte eyed my hand for just a moment before she grabbed it and shook. "It looks like the Adler sisters are going into business together."

"Into business together?" I scoffed, ignoring her use of

our mother's maiden name. Neither of us used it. Her last name was Ray. Our mother had left both of us, so I wasn't sure why Charlotte wanted to claim that name. If she wanted to change her surname, she should take Dad's since he'd raised her. But that was her business. I was just about to reiterate that we were in no way business partners and that she was working for me when Charlotte laughed, cutting me off.

"Relax, Marion. I don't want to be in charge of anything other than myself. Stress causes too many wrinkles." She leaned in, studying my face. "But it looks like you already know that."

"You're a jerk," I said without any heat.

"Right back at ya, big sis." She winked.

We grinned at each other. And for the first time since Charlotte rolled into town, I started to think that maybe, just maybe, it was a good thing she'd come.

Dad held up his drink and said, "A toast to my two favorite girls."

We all toasted and then ordered dessert.

Once we were all finished and Dad paid the bill, he cleared his throat and said, "I think maybe now is a good time to talk."

Tensing, I ignored the sudden nerves that had taken up residence in my stomach. He looked far too serious, and although I had no idea what he was about to say, I somehow just knew I wasn't going to like it.

"We're listening, Dad," Charlotte said.

He glanced once at Tazia and then squared his shoulders as he gave us his full attention. "I got a phone call."

Charlotte and I both waited for him to continue.

His gaze was steady on the two of us when he said, "It's your mother. She knows Charlotte is here, and she's decided she wants to see you both. She has... news."

"You talked to mom?" I asked automatically, shock making my body go numb. "When?"

"This morning," he said.

"Is she sick?" Charlotte asked, pressing her hand to the base of her throat.

He shook his head. "It's not my news to tell, but I did want to warn you that she'll be here within the next few days."

The nerves in my stomach turned to a ball of anxiety. I hadn't seen my mother in years. We were no contact for a reason. "Why did she call you and not one of us?"

He sighed. "Because, Marion, of the three of us, I'm the only one currently talking to her."

Dad was talking to Mom? As in he'd been in contact with her before this morning? Confusion swirled in my mind, making me frown. "Wait." I turned to my sister. "You're not talking to her either?"

Charlotte shook her head. "We had a bit of a falling-out over a fireman and his dog."

"Now there's a story. What happened? Did one of you try to steal the man's puppy or something?"

She snorted. "If only. Minx and I met him and his chihuahua at the dog park and were making plans for a playdate when she inserted herself and started flirting with him shamelessly. About the time she had a wardrobe malfunction, he hightailed it out of there and I haven't seen him since. The neighborhood gossip told me he switched dog parks."

"Well, that's... interesting," Tazia said.

"You can say that again," Charlotte and I said at the same time. We glanced at each other and started laughing.

By the time we left the restaurant, I was filled with gratitude for my dad, sister, and Tazia. And I'd *almost* managed to put my mother out of my mind. Almost, but not quite.

CHAPTER 6

"*N*ow that's some serious man-candy," Charlotte said as I pulled my SUV into my driveway.

I glanced around, looking for whoever she was ogling. "Where?"

"Your front porch." Charlotte jumped out of the vehicle and walked over to Jax, who was leaning against one of the porch pillars. His handsome face was aglow from the porch light. "Hey, handsome."

"Good evening, Charlotte," Jax said, sounding impatient with her.

"Now don't be so surly. You'll get used to me eventually," she said sweetly. "Especially now that Marion and I are working together."

"You are?" His eyebrows rose nearly to his hairline as he met my gaze.

I gave him a weak smile. Jax and Charlotte hadn't exactly gotten off on the right foot. Between her dog trying to eat him every time he walked into the house and Charlotte always shamelessly flirting with him, his patience was running out. "I'll tell you all about it over coffee."

"It's going to have to wait until morning," Jax said. "I was just waiting to let you know I'm going to stay at my place tonight." He glanced at the front door and scowled. "That dog isn't in the mood for guests."

"Charlotte," I said with a sigh. "You're going to have to kennel her while we're not here if she can't get used to Jax. Or at least keep her in the guest room."

My sister placed a hand over her heart and gave me a look that indicated she was horrified by my suggestion. "I'm *not* caging my baby."

"A kennel is not a cage," I insisted. "Dogs that are kennel trained actually love them and feel safe in them. Besides, it's not like she'd be in there all the time. Just when you aren't here."

"No way, Marion," she said, glowering at me. "Minx isn't going to be locked up." She huffed and reached for the door knob.

"Charlotte." I placed my hand on her arm, not sure why I was trying to stop her. I needed to talk to Jax, and she needed to deal with her dog. But after the progress we'd made on our relationship earlier in the day, I just wanted to make sure we didn't take a step backward due to a disagreement about her dog.

"What?" She glanced back at me, feigning annoyance. It was enough to tell me we were fine and she was just putting on a show. But her expression quickly changed to one of confusion as she looked between me and Jax. "Wait a minute here. You two don't have matching purple auras."

I bit back an annoyed sigh. One benefit to losing my aura-reading ability was that I didn't have to be reminded that Jax and I weren't a perfect match. At least not according to our auras. It was one of the reasons it took us so long to get together. I was convinced we were doomed. But once I moved to Premonition Pointe and found that Jax was divorced, the mutual attraction we'd always had for each other had been too much to ignore.

"Our aura colors aren't important," Jax said, his tone full of confidence.

"The hell they aren't." Charlotte frowned at me. Then she lowered her voice, sounding concerned for me. "You know this isn't going to last, right?"

"Charlotte, leave it alone," I said. "Not every love match has matching auras."

She blinked and then shook her head. While eyeing him up and down, she said, "Well, I guess if I was banging someone who looked like him, I'd be telling myself that, too."

Before I could reply, she opened the door and Minx ran outside and straight for Jax.

"Son of a bitch!" he yelled and leaped out of the way before she could get her pound of flesh.

"No, no, baby girl," Charlotte said mildly as she calmly scooped up the chihuahua and cuddled her against her chest.

Minx bared her teeth and growled in Jax's direction.

Charlotte just chuckled, scratched the dog behind her ears, and disappeared into the house.

A pulse twitched in Jax's jaw as he stared at the closed door. "You know, this is the first time I've ever had a dog have such a visceral reaction to me. Normally they eat up my ear scratches and belly rubs, and If that doesn't work, then excessive bribery with various treats usually does the trick."

"I know. There's a reason Paris Francine loves you so much," I said helpfully.

He blew out a breath. "I just can't stay here with a dog that's determined to rip my balls off. I can't even get up in the middle of the night for water since, if last night is any indication, Charlotte is going to be up at all hours."

Disappointment skittered through me, but I could hardly argue. I wouldn't want to stay in a hostile environment either. "How about I pack a bag and come spend the night with you?"

His eyes lit with interest. "Now that sounds like a plan. Meet you back at my place?"

"I'll be right behind you." Leaning in, I pressed a long, lingering kiss to his lips. Heat surged through my veins, and I wanted to wrap myself around him, soak up his warmth, and revel in his strong arms and muscular body.

Jax let out a tiny groan as he pulled away from me. "I am about five seconds from carrying you into your bedroom."

The passion between us had always been like this. The raw hunger that we felt for each other never faded. My body craved his and his craved mine. That fact used to scare me a little. I'd always felt like I was just waiting for the honeymoon period of our relationship to wear off and suddenly we'd be nothing more than two people who were going through the motions of a relationship. Without that aura connection, what would we become? I still had those doubts every once in a while, but the truth was, I was tired of being afraid. All I could do was love him in the moment and believe that against the odds, we'd make it.

I placed my hand on his chest and gently pushed him away just far enough that I could catch my breath. "It's better for all of us if we have our privacy at your place. Go on, now. I'll only be a few minutes."

He stepped back into my space, buried his hand in my hair, and gave me a rough kiss before quickly releasing me and walking to his truck parked at the curb. "I'll have the wine ready."

My head was spinning, and there was a smile claiming my lips as I found my way into my house.

"Gah! I hate you right now," Charlotte exclaimed, standing in the kitchen doorway and giving me a look of disgust.

"Um, why?" I asked her, confused.

"It's not fair. You have everything. This house, your business, a lot of friends, and a man who is so hot it's a wonder your lips aren't scorched." With her dog tucked in one arm, she spun on her heel and disappeared into the other room.

A second later, the sound of glass crashing to the floor had me gritting my teeth and following her.

"What happened?" I asked, staring at my favorite midnight blue ceramic mug that had a picture of a gold broom and a woman in a witch hat that said, *Yes, I can drive a stick.* It was now shattered into hundreds of pieces on the tiled floor.

"I'm so sorry. I didn't see it there. I swear," she said, holding her free hand up. Minx was wiggling around, desperate to get out of her hold. Charlotte grabbed her dog with both hands, nearly losing her grip on the small pup. "I'm gonna have to take her into my room until we get this cleaned up."

"That sounds like a plan," I said, muttering to myself about the cost of the handmade mug. I went to work on making sure every last tiny shard of the ruined mug was swept up. Once I was done, I hurried into my room, threw some clothes in a bag, and headed for the front door.

Minx ran out of the guest room, straight for me, her little tail wagging so hard I wondered if she might throw her back out. Unable to resist, I scooped her up and gave her smooches on her head. "You're such a good girl," I told her. "Though I do wish you didn't hate my boyfriend so much. He doesn't deserve all that vitriol, you know."

The tail-wagging stopped, and the dog gave me a look that screamed skepticism.

I couldn't help the laugh that bubbled up from the back of my throat. "You are a character."

"She's never been wrong about someone before," Charlotte said.

I glanced up, finding my sister leaning against the couch, studying me.

"You should probably look twice at Jax if Minx hates him so much."

I carefully put Minx down on the floor and gave my sister a flat stare. "Why are you trying to cause a rift between me and Jax?"

"What?" she scoffed. "I'm doing no such thing."

I blew out an irritated breath. "Oh, no? First you went on and on about how our auras aren't a match... right in front of him, I might add. And now you're telling me that a six-pound chihuahua, a breed that is known for being very particular about who they like and don't like, should suddenly make me suspicious of him. I've known Jax for a very long time, Charlotte. There's nothing to 'look twice at' when it comes to him. I think I'll trust my own judgment on this one."

"Okay," she said agreeably. "I'm just trying to look out for you. But if you say there's nothing to worry about, I'll let it go." She moved toward the kitchen again. Just as I was opening the front door, she called over her shoulder, "Sorry about the mug. And thanks for cleaning it up. I owe you one."

"No you don't," I said. "Family doesn't owe family."

A genuine smile lit her pretty face. "I like that. You know what, Marion?"

"What's that?"

"It's good to feel like I'm finally home." She nodded once and ducked into the kitchen.

My heart seemed to swell just a little bit. It was good to have her back.

CHAPTER 7

*J*ax's house was dark, but the porch light was on when I pulled into the driveway next to his truck. I smiled to myself, knowing he was likely waiting for me in his bedroom. Or maybe the shower. The anticipation of being in his arms made me hurry to the front door. I knocked softly, but when he didn't answer, I pulled out the key he'd given me and let myself in.

The house was quiet as I made my way to the bedroom. Light shone from beneath his door. "Jax?"

He didn't answer.

The door creaked slightly as I pushed it open, finding his bed made and light coming from the bathroom. The faint drum of the water from the shower had me quickly pulling my clothes off. A moment later, I opened the glass shower door and let myself in. Slipping my arms around his waist, I pressed myself to his back and said, "Hey, sexy."

He leaned into me and let out a contented sigh. "I was hoping you'd get here before the water turned cold."

"Me, too."

Jax turned and took my mouth, kissing me hungrily.

I buried my hands in his hair and held on as my body heated from the inside out. My hunger for him was nearly insatiable.

His hands roamed down my back and cupped my butt cheeks, pulling me tighter to his rock-hard body that was warm from the shower. It had taken me all of 2.5 seconds to go from *I want* you to *I need you. Now.*

"Jax," I said, my voice husky. "I… Holy mother-effing son of a bitch!" The water had suddenly turned ice cold, and we both jumped out of the shower spray.

"Dammit!" Jax shut the water off and quickly grabbed a towel to wrap around my shoulders. He ran a frustrated hand through his dark damp hair and shook his head. "That shouldn't have happened."

"How long have you been in here?" I asked, my teeth chattering. It was late April on the California coast. While it wasn't exactly winter weather, it wasn't warm, either, and a cold shower was the last thing we'd needed.

"Not that long." He ushered me out of the shower, quickly dried off, and pulled his clothes back on. "Turn the fireplace on if you want. I'm going to go check on the water heater."

"Sure." With my skin covered in gooseflesh, I dried as best I could, wrapped myself in his oversized robe, and then went to find the gas fireplace control. The fire flared to life, and I stood there for a moment, basking in the warmth of the flames.

I heard swearing from the other side of the house. That wasn't a good sign. Sighing, I found my way into the kitchen and made a couple of cups of hot chocolate. By the time I was done, I found Jax lying in bed, staring up at the ceiling.

"What's the verdict?"

"It has power, and the breaker isn't tripped. It's likely a bad element. I'll see about fixing it tomorrow." He pulled the covers back, inviting me in. "Come here. I want to warm you up."

I slid in and handed him one of the mugs. He took a sip and grinned. "Did you put a little Irish cream in this?"

"I figured we could use it." I pressed a soft kiss to his lips and closed my eyes as he ran his hand down my neck, lightly kneading my muscles. "That is incredible."

"Um-hmm," he mumbled.

I glanced over at my boyfriend, finding his eyes closed and the mostly full mug of hot chocolate on his nightstand. His hand slipped from my neck as his breathing turned deeper, steadier.

Sighing, I finished off my spiked hot chocolate, got up and brushed my teeth, turned off the fireplace and the lights, then slipped back into bed next to Jax. What we'd started in the shower would just have to wait until morning.

GRAY MORNING LIGHT filtered into the room as I blinked awake. The stillness of the morning told me it was early, and I rolled to my side, reaching for Jax, only to find the bed cool and empty. Frowning, I glanced around the room.

There was no sign of him.

I sat up and glanced at the clock. It was just before six. It wasn't necessarily unusual for Jax to get up that early. Sometimes he liked to get a jump on projects, especially if they were commercial builds, but if we spent the night together, he almost never got up without at least a quick round of morning sex. That's just the way it was between us.

Rubbing my eyes, I dragged myself out of bed, wrapped myself in his robe, and went to find him.

"Hey," I said when I spotted him at the table behind his laptop.

Jax glanced up, his eyes tired. "Hey. Sorry. Did I wake you?"

"No." I slid into the chair next to him and took a sip of his coffee, only to grimace when I realized it was cold. "How long have you been up?"

"A few hours." He nodded to the mug. "Sorry about that. I guess I got caught up in my computer files."

"I guess so."

Jax rose and went to the coffee pot, where he got me a fresh cup. After doctoring it the way I liked, he handed it to me, kissed me on the top of my head, and said, "I've got an early appointment. Call you later?"

"Sure." I watched him retreat to the bedroom. A few minutes later, I heard the soft sound of his front door opening and closing, followed by the rumble of his truck. Frowning, I took my mug to the sink, rinsed it in the ice-cold water and then got dressed. There was no denying I was disappointed by the morning's interaction. And while I missed his body, that wasn't the problem. He'd just seemed... different. A little bit distant, and I wasn't sure why.

There was something on his mind. I just didn't know what it was.

Surely he'd tell me when he was ready. Right? A feeling of unease settled in my gut. Was something off with us? Or was it just Jax? I bit my bottom lip and shook my head. One off morning didn't mean our relationship was going south.

Get a grip, Marion, I told myself. If a client had come to me with worries about this morning's interaction, I'd tell her she was overreacting and that if her partner was still acting distant the next time they saw each other, to just talk to him.

And that's exactly what I'd do. But that intention did nothing to ease the sense that something was just off.

Shaking my head, I got dressed and headed home where a hot shower and a tiny ball of puppy energy was waiting for me.

CHAPTER 8

"Good morning, sunshine," Charlotte said when I walked into the kitchen after a long hot shower.

"Morning," I muttered and reached for the coffee pot.

"Wow. That doesn't sound chipper. I thought a night with your construction man would've put a big smile on your face. What happened? Did he finish without taking care of you first?" She laughed, making it clear she was only teasing.

"We didn't even get that far," I said, taking a long sip of my gloriously rich caramel-cream-flavored coffee. "I guess you could say that the water heater literally put a freeze on our plans when it suddenly gave out. After we warmed up, Jax sort of just passed out and then he had to go to work early this morning."

"You mean he didn't rally?" She shook her head sadly. "It must suck to get old."

I chuckled. "There are some perks, but I'll agree with you on that one."

Charlotte walked over to the pantry, rummaged around for a second, and then held up a box of Pop-Tarts. "I think you deserve a treat this morning. If you can't have sex, then this is the next best thing."

I had to give it to her, she had a point.

"Eat up," she said, placing the toasted Pop-Tarts in front of me. "After you snarf these down, I'm taking you to the spa."

"You are?"

"Yep. I made an appointment for a full morning of beauty treatments. If you're going to find me the man of my dreams, then I'm going to look my best. I'll just tell Lance to make room for one more."

"I'm not sure…" But before I could get my thoughts out, she was already on the phone, charming the owner of the Liminal Day Spa.

"Now, Lance. Surely you have room for Premonition Pointe's prized matchmaker," she said sweetly. "You do realize that she sends all her clients to you when they're in the market for a makeover, right?"

She paused, giving me two thumbs up. "Perfect," she said into the phone. "I really appreciate this. And don't you worry, we'll be sure to tip generously. I know it's not easy to fit someone in last minute."

They chatted about a few more details before Charlotte ended the call and gave me a cheeky grin. "I'm an excellent people person. Just wait. Your clients are going to love me."

If she handled them like she had Lance, I had no doubt

about that. "You could always charm your way out of anything. I'm ready when you are."

"Let me just take Minx out one more time."

"I DON'T THINK I have been this relaxed since Mom took me on a trip to an exclusive spa up in Napa," Charlotte said, sighing with pleasure.

Even the mention of my mother couldn't bring me down. Not this time. We were sitting side by side in reclining chairs, with one technician giving us facials while massage therapists worked their magic on our feet. I wasn't sure how Charlotte was paying for this, but she'd insisted the entire trip was on her as a way of repaying me for letting her stay at my house. I wasn't complaining. "It is pretty spectacular. When did you go to Napa with Mom?"

I knew Charlotte had been in touch with our mother at some point after she'd left us ten years ago. Dad had mentioned it while trying to get me and Charlotte to reconnect. I'd declined. My life had just been so much more peaceful without dealing with Mom's drama.

"Hmm, about a year ago, I guess." Charlotte rolled her eyes. "I should've known the trip had everything to do with some guy she was seeing. I swear, you haven't lived until your mother puts a sock on the hotel room door to signal she's in there getting her groove on."

My eyes widened. "You can't be serious."

"Oh, I am. I should have left her butt there, but since I was the one who drove us, I felt too guilty to leave her stranded. It was six weeks later when she went after the fireman I'd made friends with, and shortly after that I told her I needed my space. It was just the straw that broke the camel's back, you know? I haven't spoken to her since." She waved a hand in the air as if to dispel any negative energy. "Anyway, enough about that. What do you think she wants to tell us?"

I shrugged one shoulder. "Maybe she's getting married again."

Charlotte visibly shuddered. "Ugh. You haven't met the men she usually dates. I swear, Dad was the only good one. The rest..." She wrinkled her nose, causing her green face mask to crack. "Loser city. So I hope that's not it. I don't want to be guilted into wearing an ugly bridesmaid dress just to watch her make another mistake."

"Yeah, I wouldn't be excited about that either, but you never know. She did pick a good one once before," I said, trying to be diplomatic. There were so many hard feelings when it came to our mother. Sometimes it helped to vent. Other times, like now, it was just making everything worse. I didn't want to think about her or why she was requesting to see us. All I wanted was to enjoy my time with my sister. It had been a very long time since we'd been in a good space together. I didn't want to ruin it.

She snorted. "Yeah, maybe. I'm not holding my breath."

I gave her a small smile and reached over to squeeze her hand. She returned the gesture as tears shone in her big green eyes. She quickly blinked them back and let out a soft chuckle. "Look at me, getting all sentimental because my big sister is being nice to me."

"Well, there's a first time for everything," I joked.

"It's because that strong masseuse worked that ache out of the bottom of your feet, isn't it?" she said, eyeing the man still working on my calf.

"Yes." I nodded, but then in a softened tone I added, "And also because I'm having fun and enjoying having my little sister back in town."

"Even though I barged in on you?" she challenged.

"You wouldn't be you if you hadn't." I winked at her. "Now, shhh. I'm trying to relax."

Her lips twitched, and there was a happy sparkle in her eyes as she laid back and let out a contented sigh.

"I don't think life gets better than this," I said to Charlotte as we started to make our way to the dressing room forty-five minutes later. "I've been rubbed, scrubbed, waxed, and pampered to the point that I think I might be boneless."

"Me too. Isn't it fantastic?" Charlotte positively glowed and radiated beauty.

"Oh, to be twenty-eight again," I said with a wistful sigh.

"Why the hell would you want to be my age?" she scoffed. "Life at fifty looks to be pretty spectacular from where I'm sitting."

"I'm not fifty," I said, making it sound like I was offended. "Yet."

"Close enough. But let's look at the facts. You have an adorable house, a successful business, a hot boyfriend, a tight-knit group of friends, and an amazing little sister. What more do you need?"

I laughed. "You're right. All of that is wonderful. But it

wouldn't hurt to have your tight ass, smooth skin, and fewer wrinkles."

"Plastic surgery will fix all that if you care that much."

That was just it. I didn't. Not really. Sure, I tried to take care of my skin and pretended to go on diets when I wasn't shoving Pop-Tarts in my face, but the thought of going under the knife to improve the shell I was living in made me shudder. "No thanks. I'm good."

"I thought you'd say that. But if you ever want to minimize those wrinkles, I'm sure Lance can point you in the right direction."

"True. And I think Gigi has some sort of miracle cream that—"

"When did the outbreak start?" a woman asked a man as they rounded the corner in the hallway.

"Two nights ago. I was at a bar in town when I just suddenly broke out into hives. I don't know if it was a reaction to something I drank or what, but I took antihistamines, tried a cream from the healer, and even made a sacrifice to the goddess, but nothing worked."

"Sacrifice?" Charlotte and I and the technician all said at once.

The man glanced up at me and Charlotte, appearing startled.

"Sorry, I said quickly. We were just on the way to the locker rooms and couldn't help overhearing."

He covered his splotchy red face with his hands and shook his head. "It's fine, I guess. I just... would rather not have people seeing me this way."

"That's understandable," the technician said, gently

guiding him into one of the empty rooms before we heard what exactly he'd sacrificed in an attempt to cure his hives.

Charlotte and I didn't move. I knew we were both thinking the same thing. It was highly likely that his rash was caused by her curse.

"We can't leave until we talk to him," I said.

"But there's nothing I can do," she whispered, fear flickering in her eyes.

"Maybe not, but we still need to talk to him, find out if he was at Hallucinations, how bad his symptoms are, and see if there's something we can do. I can call the coven together. They might be able to break the curse."

She bit down on her bottom lip and glanced at the locker room and then back at the treatment room where the man was with the technician. "You really think we might be able to do something to help him?"

"We won't know unless we try."

The door started to open and I hurried Charlotte into the locker room. But we stayed close to the entrance so that I could watch the man's room.

"Let me just get our hive healing kit and I'll be right back," the tech said.

"Go now." Charlotte nudged me.

"No. Not yet. We don't have enough time. Go get changed while I keep an eye out."

Charlotte did as I asked and was back just as the tech slipped into his room again. "Now you," she said, nudging me. "I'll let you know if the tech leaves again."

I hesitated for just a moment, but then hurried over to my locker and stuffed myself back into my clothes. I didn't want to be half naked while trying to get details from the man. Besides, if we got caught bothering someone while they got a procedure, we might need to hightail it out of there quickly.

"The tech just left. She said something about being back in ten minutes." Charlotte grabbed my hand and pulled me after her. For someone who'd been reluctant to even talk to the man, she seemed pretty determined now.

"What's with the change of heart?" I asked her.

"If you think we can break the curse, then I'm all in. Plus, you know, I don't feel all that great about cursing the man."

"Fair enough."

We crept into the hallway, careful to make sure no one saw us, and then quickly slipped into the man's room. Charlotte closed the door quietly behind us.

"Has it been ten minutes already?" the man asked. He was lying on the table on his back with a white towel covering his face. "Are my hives gone yet?"

His hives didn't look like any hives I'd seen before. If you asked me, he was having a severe acne breakout.

"Um, no to both questions?" Charlotte said, making her answer sound like a question.

"Is there another procedure?" he asked, starting to sit up.

I placed a light hand on him, urging him to lie back down. "No. We're just here to ask you some questions."

The man removed the towel and peeked up at us. His face was covered with a clear cream that made his skin look shiny. "You're the two women from the hallway, right?"

"Yes," I said. There was no point in denying it.

"What are you doing in here?" This time he did sit up as he studied both of us warily.

"I'm so sorry to interrupt you, but I was just hoping you could answer some questions for us about the... *hives*. You see, we have a friend who is having the same symptoms, and we're hoping to find a way to help them out." It was just a small white lie, right? Though I supposed Charlotte would like to break the curse she'd cast on Eli.

"You do? Was he at Hallucinations night before last?" the man asked.

"Yes," Charlotte and I said at the same time. My sister let out a nervous chuckle. "My friend has a rash all over his face that looks similar to yours."

"And he hasn't been able to clear it either?" The man slumped, looking completely dejected.

"Not yet," Charlotte said and then looked at me helplessly.

I cleared my throat. "Uh, do you mind telling us how severe your outbreak is?"

"How severe?" He looked at me like I'd lost my mind. "Just look at me. The hives are everywhere. Not just my face either. My hands, my feet, my..." he glanced down at his crotch before he averted his gaze. "Let's just say it's in most of my sensitive areas."

"Oh my goddess," Charlotte said, covering her mouth. "I'm so sorry."

"Yeah, so am I," he said, sounding dejected. "That blood sacrifice I tried only managed to make it hard to type." He held up his left hand, showing his index finger that was wrapped in a bandage.

"Oh, thank goodness." Charlotte pressed a hand to her chest. "The sacrifice was just blood from your finger."

"Of course it was. What did you think? That I'd tracked down a virgin and held a séance by the light of the full moon?" He snorted as if that were preposterous.

"Well, no, not exactly," Charlotte said carefully. "But there are some really strange people in this world."

"Oh my gods." The man looked scandalized. "Maybe so, but I'm not one of them."

"We know," I said soothingly and then frowned as I peered at his face. "Um, Mister…"

"Waters. Bradley Waters. And you are?" he asked, eyebrows raised.

"I'm Marion, and this is my sister, Charlotte," I said, watching in horror as the hives beneath his face mask seemed to start swelling.

Charlotte's eyes widened to the size of saucers. "Mr. Waters, I think it's time for you to see a doctor."

"What? Why?" He jumped off the table and rushed to the mirror hanging on the wall. He let out a cry and quickly moved to the small hand sink and started splashing water on his face. "Help me get it off," he cried. "Get this mask off me."

"I can help," Charlotte said, grabbing a fresh towel from a small stack and wetting it with the water. "Here. Hold still."

"Hurry," Bradley demanded, panic in his tone.

I rushed to get another towel and started to help Charlotte, each of us taking one side of his face, both being careful to wipe away the mask but not irritate his skin further.

"Is it off?" he demanded.

"Just need to do one more section," I said and reached for his chin.

Charlotte's hand collided with mine, and suddenly my hand started to tingle.

"What's that?" Charlotte asked, staring at the light shimmering around our hands.

"Magic," I whispered, my eyes wide as I watched it start to crawl over Bradley.

Charlotte tried to yank her hand back and grunted when it didn't budge. She struggled, frantically trying to get away from both of us, but I placed my free hand on her arm and said, "Stop struggling, Char. Look."

She blinked rapidly and then focused on the man's face. The magic had engulfed him, but more importantly, the hives covering his face were shrinking and the bridge of his nose started to clear.

"What's happening to me?" the man asked, his voice slightly muffled by the magic bubble encasing him.

"We're healing you," I said and smiled when his entire body was engulfed in the light. I had no way of knowing if he was suffering from erectile dysfunction like the blonde's husband had been, but hopefully, if the magic was curing his breakout it would cure any issues with his other parts, too.

Just as suddenly as the magic had appeared, it vanished, leaving all three of us standing there staring at each other.

The door swung open, and the technician walked in with a basket of warm towels. She frowned at us. "What's going on in here? This is a private— Oh, excellent. The mask worked," she said, a huge smile on her face. "I'll be honest, I wasn't entirely sure that was going to work."

"It didn't," Bradley said, holding his hand out for one of the towels.

"What do you mean?" she asked as she handed one to him. "The hives are gone. Did they come back somewhere else?"

A look of horror crossed over his face, and right there in front of all three of us, he pulled his robe open and then peeked in his boxer briefs at his crotch. He let out a huge sigh of relief. "No. No it didn't. It's gone."

"It seems to work, too, judging by that sizable bulge," Charlotte said, giving him a nod of approval.

His face turned bright red. "I've never had any complaints before."

Charlotte winked. "I bet you haven't."

"Uh, does someone want to explain to me what's going on?" the tech asked.

"I've got it from here," a man said from the doorway.

I glanced over and spotted Lance, the tall, dark-skinned owner of the spa.

The tech nodded and quickly departed the room. She stopped briefly at Lance's side. "I'm sorry about this. I won't let it happen again."

He jerked his head, indicating that she should go.

"These ladies cured me," Bradley said the moment Lance stepped in and closed the door. "I don't know what they did, but I came in here looking for this rash to go away, and now it's gone. That's all that matters to me."

"That's excellent." Lance moved to lean against the counter. "I'm glad you're a satisfied customer."

"More than satisfied," he said with a definitive nod. "Now if you don't mind, I'm going to go get dressed and get on with my day."

"Let us know if we can be of any other service to you," the spa owner said and then thanked him for coming in.

Bradley glanced back at me and Charlotte. "Thank you. You have no idea how much I appreciate this."

"You're welcome," I said with an easy smile.

Charlotte said nothing. It must've felt strange to be thanked for fixing the curse she was responsible for unleashing on the poor unsuspecting man.

Once the door clicked shut, Lance said, "Well. That was quite interesting. Care to share what happened in here?"

"I'm not really sure," I hedged. It was the truth. I didn't know how magic just started pouring out of us or why it had cured Bradley.

"I cursed him," Charlotte blurted.

Lance's brows shot up. "Why?"

I almost laughed at the way Lance seemed not at all shocked. Like it was perfectly normal for a woman to curse a man and then sneak into a spa to help cure him. I mean, cursing a man seemed completely normal as long as he deserved it. It was the reversing part that was the more interesting story.

"I didn't do it on purpose." Charlotte sat heavily on the procedure table. "It was a complete accident, and not even directed at him or the rest of the men in the bar. I just... I guess I don't know how to control my own magic."

"Oh, girl," Lance said, shaking his head with an amused smile on his face. "Are you seriously telling me that you cursed an entire bar full of men with acne?"

"I thought he had hives," Charlotte said. "Do hives look like pimples? I've never had them."

"No, they don't. That man had severe acne. On his face, his neck, his shoulders, and even his man parts. He just didn't want to call it that, so we went with hives. No wonder he was having trouble getting it up." Lance held his hand up, waiting for her to give him a high five.

Charlotte tentatively reached out and tapped his hand.

Lance threw his head back and laughed. "Honey, if you only knew how many times I've wished I could curse a bar full of men. They can be downright hideous sometimes, can't they?"

"The one I was trying to spell wasn't being terrible, but I do get your point. Sometimes, they make me want to tear their hair out."

"Or give them broken penis's," Lance said with a snort.

"So he did have ED," I said far too enthusiastically.

Lance chuckled. "Is that ever a reason for celebration?"

"No, not at all," I said, feeling my face flush. "It's just that the acne and the ED appear to be common symptoms for all of Charlotte's victims."

"Oh gods." Charlotte covered her face. "I can't believe this. I'm a walking disaster. I think I need a keeper."

"That's what I'm here for," I said, patting her back. Magic zipped through my fingertips the moment I touched her, though as soon as I pulled my hand away, it vanished.

"Wow," Lance said. "I don't know what's going on here,

Miss Marion, but it looks like you and your sister have some serious power building between you. Do you mind if I call you in if we get another case of *hives* with a side of ED?"

"No, not at all. Though I'm not sure we could replicate whatever happened here today," I said. "Neither one of us really understood what was happening until it was over."

"Oh, I think you can. Remember, most magic is all about the intention." Lance pulled the door open. "Come with me to the front desk so I can get your number and comp your visit today."

"You don't have to do that," I said, but I quickly clamped my mouth shut when Charlotte cleared her throat suggestively. Oops. I should've kept quiet since I wasn't even the one who was supposed to be paying for this little adventure.

"I know, but I want to." Lance pressed his hand to the small of Charlotte's back and then mine before leading us back out to the lobby.

CHAPTER 9

*A*fter the spa, Charlotte and I grabbed some sandwiches and headed into the office.

"I can't believe this is my first day," my sister said as she sat at my desk, poking at the computer keys. "What do you want me to do? File something? Make you coffee? Grab your dry cleaning?" She wrinkled her nose. "Maybe not that. Dry cleaners always smell so... chemically."

All I could do was laugh. "First of all, do I look like I frequent the dry cleaner very often?" I was dressed in jeans and a light sweater. It wasn't what I'd wear to a mixer, but the office was pretty casual. There was no need to be wearing a suit and heels all day when I mostly responded to clients through email or Facetime chats.

"You probably could use a wardrobe upgrade," she said thoughtfully as she kicked her feet up and rested them on my desk. "You're dressed to be a box store greeter."

"What?" I demanded. "I am not. Am I wearing a blue vest and horribly ugly, black orthopedic shoes?"

"No, but—"

"Nope. No, no, no, no, no, no, nope! I'm dressed for business casual. There is nothing wrong with clean jeans, a nice sweater, and cute shoes."

Charlotte glanced down at my canvas sneakers that had a repeating puppy pattern on them. "I think we need to work on your understanding of age-appropriate clothing."

"Oh, come on. These are adorable." I sat in a chair next to her and propped my foot up beside hers. "Puppies with their tongues out. Super cute. Admit it."

"Fine." She put both her feet back on the floor. "Super cute, but they still aren't appropriate for the office. With those jeans and that sweater, the look would be much better with a pair of knee-high boots."

"That's... yeah, okay. You have a point." I had to give her that one. My shoes did put me squarely into weekend casual. "It doesn't matter though. We don't have any appointments today."

A knock sounded on the door just before a familiar man in a formfitting suit walked in.

Charlotte sucked in a sharp breath and fanned herself, making no effort to hide her appreciation for the man.

I stood and strode over, holding my arms out. "Brix. What brings you here today?"

The tall blond man leaned down and gave me a hug. "I was in town and thought I'd stop by to see my favorite matchmaker."

Pulling back, I eyed him with suspicion. "What exactly is

a special agent from the Magical Task Force doing in Premonition Pointe? Please don't tell me that someone is missing. They aren't, are they?" I pressed a hand to my temple, fighting off the instant headache that always formed when I thought about the events that went down in my hometown just a few short months ago when an old friend and Kennedy had been abducted. Ice ran down my spine, making me shiver.

"No, no. Nothing like that," he said easily. "Just following a lead on a case I've been working on for a while. Nothing you need to be worried about."

"Magical Task Force?" Charlotte asked, sounding like a timid five-year-old.

Could she sound any guiltier? I highly doubted Brix, a high-level agent at the MTF, was in town because of her accidental cursing down at Hallucinations. But it had affected a high-profile actor, so it was better if we just kept our mouths shut. "Brix, I'd like you to meet my sister, Charlotte."

"Charlotte, it's nice to meet you," he said, holding his hand out to her.

My sister quickly took his hand in both of hers and said, "It's really nice to meet you. It's not every day a girl meets an actual god."

"God?" Brix looked over at me and chuckled. "She's pulling my leg, right?"

"Afraid not," I said. "That's what you get for being so damned good looking."

If Charlotte was going to play the flirt to distract him, then I was all in on the game.

"Stop," he said, shaking his head. But then he grinned and played along. "You two are making me blush."

"Come sit down right here, Brix," Charlotte said, leading him to the chair opposite my desk. "Tell me, do you have a girlfriend?"

"Well, no—" he started.

"Are you dating anyone?"

"Why? Are you asking me out?" he teased.

"Would you say yes if I did?" Charlotte twisted one of her locks, really laying it on thick.

"Definitely. Drinks? Dinner? A weekend away in the Caribbean?"

Charlotte snorted. "You really know how to woo a girl, don't you?"

"I try." The smugness in his expression really was something to be admired.

"But I can't date you," Charlotte said regrettably. "It would be unethical."

I frowned, wondering where she was going with that. The age difference? Brix was in his early fifties, while Charlotte was only twenty-eight. And while that was quite the age gap, that didn't mean it would be unethical to date. Or at least it wouldn't if she hadn't been casting illegal compulsion spells while he was busy tracking down people who abused their powers.

"Why's that?" he asked, tilting his head with interest.

"Because you're going to be my very first client. Marion just brought me on as a partner, and I can't think of a better first client than the most handsome man I've seen in maybe... ever."

"You're working with Marion now?" he asked curiously. "Partners?"

"Something like that," she said with a wink.

Brix met my gaze, and I gave him a tiny shake of my head. "We're seeing how things go."

"Anyway." Charlotte tapped a key to wake up the computer, even though I knew she had no idea how to use my systems. "What do you say, Brix? Are you ready to find your dream girl?"

"What if I already have?" he asked, letting his gaze roam over her body.

Charlotte shook her index finger at him. "Behave now. I already explained it would be unethical for me to date a client."

"I haven't committed to being a client, though," he said.

"But you will," she said sweetly. "Marion, when is our next mixer?"

"Thursday at Cryptic. It's a bookstore in town. We'll have wine and hors d'oeuvres. Just a typical meet and greet, only this time my client is looking for a same sex partner. Brix, any interest in dating a man?"

"Can't say I am. Or at least I haven't been yet," he said easily.

"Then maybe catch the next one," I added with a fake pout.

"Wait, you'll have a female client there too," Charlotte said.

"Oh, really? Who?" I asked, intensely curious about what she was up to.

"Me. You said you'd find me a love match, remember?"

"Oh, right." I hadn't given much thought to finding Charlotte someone yet, mostly since we'd agreed that we'd wait until we figured out why she was accidentally cursing people. But it appeared she wanted to step up that timeline.

"In that case, I'll be there." Brix stood and turned to me. "What time should I arrive?"

I swallowed a sigh, wishing my sister had left well enough alone. Now I'd have to worry about him finding out she'd put a pox on half the town. "Six."

"I'm looking forward to it." He nodded to Charlotte and then squeezed my shoulder on the way out.

The door clicked behind him, and I turned to Charlotte. "What was that? What part of *he works for the Magical Task Force* did you not understand? Do you know what could happen if he finds out you've been illegally cursing people?"

"Yes. I know full well what happens to women who wield too much power. Especially unexpected power," she said dramatically. "But by inviting him to the mixer, we can keep an eye on him and he won't suspect us if we're encouraging him to stick around."

"He already didn't suspect us," I said, throwing my hands up in frustration. "Brix is my friend. That's the only reason he stopped by here."

"You don't know that." Charlotte was pacing now. "I mean, I'm sure he's your friend, but you don't know that's the only reason he stopped by. He could have been feeling us out, right?"

"I suppose, but I doubt it." Though he had used my agency once before as a cover when he'd been investigating Kiera's disappearance. Charlotte's theory might seem paranoid, but it wasn't that far-fetched. Was the Hallucinations curse something Brix would even work on? He was selective about his cases these days, picking and choosing which ones he personally took on. What if Damon Grant was having the curse investigated? Would he have the pull to call in Brix?

Shaking my head, I waved my hands in the air. "This is crazy-making. Fine. Keep your friends close and your enemies closer. That's a solid strategy. Just know that I don't think Brix is my enemy, and I don't want to put him in a tough position if he finds out you're ground zero for acne and erectile dysfunction."

Charlotte lifted her chin and glanced away. "Ground zero for acne and ED. You know how to make a girl feel really special. You know that, right?"

"That's what I'm here for. To help my clients build self-confidence and feel good about themselves."

She snorted and tapped a key to wake up the computer again. "If I'm going to be one of the guests of honor at that mixer Thursday, we need to find me some men."

"I suppose you're right. Scooch over. After you fill out the questionnaire, I'll let the computer run to find you some decent matches."

"You're telling me that after all these years of going on and on about your aura-reading abilities, that it's really the computer that does the work?" She tsked. "Marion, that's cheating."

"No it isn't," I said with a laugh. "It's just to start narrowing down choices. I always have to see my clients interact and, yes, check out their auras. Now, if you want to start trying to find someone, move over so I can show you the magic."

The word magic made her eyes cloud over. She stared at her fingertips and said, "I still don't know what happened back at the spa."

"I know," I said quietly. "I don't either. But when we're done here, I'll call Iris and see if she can shed some light on it for us. Okay?"

"Yeah, okay. It's not like I'm complaining. If Bradley stays cured, then that's great. I'm just afraid that if we try something like that again my magic could backfire. Then what? It'll be on both of our hands."

"We won't do anything without testing, okay?" I asked.

"Testing. Right." She closed her eyes, sucked in a deep breath, and blew it out slowly. When she opened her eyes again, she said, "Let's do this. Show me my love matches."

CHAPTER 10

"*W*hat are we doing here?" Charlotte asked me as we moved along the trail that led to the coven circle. "My lunch isn't going to hold out forever, you know."

The moon was high in the sky and there was a chill from the ocean that was just over the bluff. "We're going to talk to my coven friends about what happened back at the spa."

Charlotte stiffened. "You mean you already told them?"

I frowned at her, wondering why she was so anxious. "Yes. They know a lot more about magic than I do. Iris already knows that you accidentally cursed a bunch of people. She thought the curse would wear off. But it's obvious it hasn't... or at least not yet. But mostly I just want their take on how we managed to suddenly heal Bradley. I'm not a healer. Neither are you."

"It was probably a fluke." She stood still, not moving forward.

I tilted my head to the side, studying her. "Don't you want to be able to help the people who were harmed by the curse?"

"Of course I do." There was anger and indignation in her tone. "I just... I don't know."

"Don't know what?" I really was trying to understand her.

"I don't want to cast any more spells. I'm afraid of what might happen."

Ah. Of course. I should have already realized that. "That's why we're meeting with the coven; so we can try to fix this. You don't want to spend the rest of your life worrying that you might accidentally curse someone, do you?"

She shook her head. "I just figured I'd never cast a spell again... ever."

I reached for her hand, squeezed it, and stared down at the magic pulsing between our fingers. "See that?"

Charlotte tried to pull away, but I wouldn't let her. "Running from whatever this is won't help, Char. Trust me. Running never works. This thing that's happening with us... I don't know why or how. But since we're both witches, I think it comes with the territory that things like this are unpredictable. Witches can sometimes cause spells or curses just by thinking something. The only path forward is to learn to control our power as much as possible. Don't you think so?"

"I guess." She stared down at the clumps of grass on the path. "Sometimes I wish I was just a normal person."

I chuckled. "Haven't you figured it out yet?"

She glanced up. "Figured what out?"

"No one is normal. Everyone has their own crap to deal with. Ours is just a little more intense."

"Intense. Yeah, that's one way of putting it."

"Marion, you're already here," Carly said, smiling at us as she and Joy appeared on the path.

"Holy crap," Charlotte said under her breath. "That's Carly Preston."

Carly's clear bell-like laugh filled the air. "In the flesh."

Leaning into Charlotte, I whispered, "I told you Carly was part of the coven."

"I know, but it didn't really sink in until just now." Charlotte turned to Carly. "Wow. It's so nice to meet you. And can I just say, you're even more beautiful in person than you are on the screen. I mean, usually a person expects movie stars to maybe seem a little more normal in person, but you..." Charlotte let out a breath. "You're radiant."

Carly gave my sister a sweet smile. "That's very kind of you. Thank you. You are lovely as well. With a face like that, I'm a little surprised someone hasn't tried to recruit you for the big screen."

"Me? An actress?" Charlotte pressed a hand to her heart. "I very seriously doubt anyone would hire me. I can never even remember what day of the week it is, much less a whole script of lines. I'd probably like modeling more. Not that I think I'm thin enough for that."

"It does take some getting used to, that's for sure" Carly said. "As far as modeling goes, there are opportunities for all sizes these days, thank the goddess. Right, Joy?"

"Definitely," Joy said. "I just did a shoot for a skincare

line, and we had a variety of men and women in all sizes there."

"Really? That does seem interesting." She turned her attention to Joy. "Would you mind if I pick your brain about modeling sometime? I don't want to bother you or anything, just get an idea of where to start and maybe what to expect?"

"Sure. I'd love to. Anything for Marion's sister." Joy slipped her arm over my shoulder and gave me a sideways hug. "Marion is one of us now."

"She's a coven member?" Charlotte asked, surprised.

"Oh no," I said, waving a hand. "Joy just means—"

"I meant that we *want* her to be a coven member," Joy said, cutting me off. She chuckled softly. "Perhaps I shouldn't have brought it up in such a casual way." She turned to me. "We were going to talk to you earlier this week, but with everything you've had going on, we decided we'd invite you to our next coven meeting. Now that we're having an impromptu one, I figured it was time to let the cat out of the bag so to speak."

"Wow." Charlotte said softly. "A coven member. That's... wow."

My sister's words reflected exactly what I was feeling. When I'd come to Premonition Pointe, my only real skill was seeing auras. Since then, I'd acquired a magical dagger that seemed to enhance whatever power I had, and now I'd gained some sort of magical connection with my sister. It was all a little bit overwhelming. I met Joy's gaze. "I don't really know what to say."

"Don't say anything right now," she said. "We'll talk more

when the rest of the coven gets here. Come on. Let's go get the circle set up."

As soon as we reached the bluff overlooking the ocean, Charlotte moved to the edge and stared, transfixed by the churning waters below. I stood back, just watching her. I'd spent a lot of years not understanding my sister, and even being resentful that she'd left not only my dad, but me too. Since she'd been in Premonition Pointe, I was coming to terms with the fact that she'd had her own traumas to overcome, due to our mother. And while she had run from me and Dad as soon as she was able, it was likely she was just running from the turmoil of her young life.

Now she was here, making new connections as an adult. And while she'd been wearing her emotional armor from the moment she'd stepped into my house, that had started to fade away, leaving a vulnerable young woman who was just trying to find her way while dealing with some pretty upsetting circumstances. The fact that she was letting her guard down and leaning on me a little made my heart full. It was good to have her back.

As Carly and Joy set up a salt circle and outlined it with candles, I stepped up next to Charlotte and said, "We'll get through this together."

"Promise?"

"Promise."

Charlotte linked her pinky finger with mine. My eyes welled. An image of a scared eight-year-old standing in the driveway as our mother left for the final time flashed in my mind. I'd been just about to turn thirty and was still building my business when I'd been summoned by my mother. She'd told me she had an emergency and needed me to watch Charlotte. The two of us were still getting used to each other since I hadn't seen much of Charlotte while my parents were separated the first time. But that afternoon when I'd arrived, my mother's bags were packed, and two daughters, one still a young girl, the other a woman, watched our mother leave our family for the final time.

The memory caused a small ache in my chest. But a soul-deep connection had been made that night between those two girls. And it had happened when Charlotte slipped her pinky around mine as we stood there, both broken, yet stronger together.

"Hey," Iris said softly from behind us.

Charlotte let go of my pinky, and we both turned to find all six of the coven members had arrived. All of them except Iris had already formed a circle and held candles as if they were ready to perform a ritual.

"Hey." I nodded to the circle. "What's the plan?"

"We're going to call the goddess of witches and see if we can get an answer as to why Charlotte's magic has gone haywire."

"Um, the goddess of witches?" Charlotte asked, looking as if she wanted to run.

I grabbed her hand again, making our magical connection spark.

Iris's gaze dropped to our hands. "Wow. That's really something."

"It is." I concentrated on tamping down the magic, and the glow that encircled our fingers dimmed until I could just barely see it.

"Don't be nervous, Charlotte," Iris said, her voice soothing. "We've done this before. Calling on a goddess is very standard for us."

"That seems a little hard to believe," Charlotte said, but she followed when Iris moved back toward the circle.

Iris handed me an unlit candle. "Marion, you should take a place next to me on the circle. Charlotte, we need you to stand in the middle."

Charlotte stood stock-still as her eyes widened, and she asked, "What? Why me?"

"Because you're the one we're seeking answers for," Iris said, nodding to the circle. "The moon is full and bright. It'll be better if we get this done before the clouds roll in."

After glancing up at the sky, Charlotte took a tentative step. And then another. And another until she was finally in position.

Without any warning, Gigi Martin raised her hands in the air and said, "Goddess of witches, light our path. Give us light to guide us to your wisdom."

All seven of the white pillar candles flared to life, illuminating our faces in the dark night.

Charlotte stared as if she'd never seen a witch magically light a candle before.

"From fire and earth to air and sea, we call our goddess of witches," Gigi called. "We humbly ask for answers to the questions we seek. From our hearts and minds, we pray you grace us with your presence and knowledge and wisdom you speak. With open souls, we request that you reveal yourself, so mote it be."

"So mote it be," the coven said in unison.

A small ring of fire flared to life around Charlotte, making her gasp and take a step back. Then she took a shaky step forward again so that she didn't get singed.

"It's working," Iris whispered to me.

I had no doubt about that. Magic coated my skin, making me feel almost invincible.

"Raise your arms," Gigi called, and everyone except Charlotte put their arms up. "Raise them, Charlotte!" Gigi ordered.

This time Charlotte complied.

The wind picked up, but it wasn't cold. The surf became louder, and as a large wave crashed against the bluff, a slight mist of saltwater settled over us.

The moon seemed to put Charlotte in the spotlight as the coven chanted together in what I figured must be Latin.

Then suddenly, the wind stopped and Charlotte stood tall, blond hair replacing her red locks and fanning out around her as if it had been charged with static.

"Hecate," Gigi murmured. "Goddess," she said reverently as she performed a slight bow. Each of us followed her example as Charlotte gave us an indulgent smile. *No*, not Charlotte. *Hecate*, the goddess of witches.

"Child," she said with a nod and then glanced up at the bright full moon. Her smile became softer and more appreciative. "You've chosen your coven circle well."

"Thank you," Gigi said. "And thank you for heeding our call. We seek only answers."

Hecate gave Gigi an approving nod. "Proceed."

"Our friend Charlotte, the witch who is hosting you, has been unable to control her magic recently. Which has, unfortunately, caused some unintentional havoc. We were hoping you could help us understand why."

"It is simple, my children. Your friend has been cursed to curse people. But you already have the answers you seek. You just need to open your eyes to them. Be wary of adversaries, especially those with sway over your heart."

The wind picked up again and just like that, the small ring of fire went out, leaving us all bathed in candlelight.

Charlotte seemed to sway on her feet. She stumbled once before she regained her balance. Her gaze landed on mine. "What just happened?"

"Hecate was here," I said, my voice hoarse with emotion. The goddess of witches had just graced us with her presence. I'd heard of covens summoning her before, but the success rate was low and I'd never heard of an experience where she spoke directly to the witches who'd summoned her. She always left a cryptic message and vanished. And while the one she'd left for us appeared to be cryptic, it didn't seem that hard to decipher.

We already had the answers we sought and should be wary of adversaries who had influence over our hearts. It seemed clear as day to me that the power Charlotte and I shared would break her curse and that we needed to be wary of our mother. There was no doubt in my mind that whatever was happening to Charlotte was somehow caused by our mother.

Iris did her best to explain what had happened. Charlotte appeared to be in a state of shock. She kept shaking her head and insisting that she didn't remember anything.

"It's okay, Char. She relayed the message to us, and that's all that matters," I said. "Let's go home and get dinner. We'll decide how to move forward after we've had some food."

"I'm not really hungry," she said.

"You were before we did the summoning," I reminded her. "I'm sure once you smell dinner cooking your appetite will come back."

She didn't look convinced but nodded anyway.

Joy cleared her throat. "Uh, guys? I sort of already let the cat out of the bag."

"Which cat?" Grace Valentine asked as she collected the candles and placed them into a drawstring bag.

"The one about us planning to ask Marion to join the coven." She gave them all a nervous smile. "It just sort of fell out of my mouth."

Carly snorted. "Yep, can confirm."

"Well, what did you say, Marion?" Hope Anderson demanded with one hand on her hip and plenty of expectation in her dark gaze.

"Nothing yet, I—"

"Say yes!" all six of them chorused.

My insides turned to jelly as their outpouring of love washed over me. How had I gotten so lucky to make such good friends in my new town? Sure, Carly and I had already been friends when we lived down in LA, but that didn't guarantee her coven circle would invite me in so wholeheartedly. With a lump in my throat and a soul full of gratitude, I said, "Yes."

CHAPTER 11

"*M*om did not curse me," Charlotte insisted. "I'd know if she had."

"How?" I asked, shoving a piece of pie in my mouth. We were back at my place, sitting on the couch while eating blackberry pie that Aunt Lucy had left for us. Minx was positioned between us, watching diligently for any crumbs we might drop.

"What do you mean, how? Surely if she cursed me, I'd feel it, right?"

I shrugged. "I guess so. But what if she did it while you were sleeping? Or drunk? Or slipped it to you in something you ate or drank? I think it's impossible to know for sure. Besides, if you were cursed, then someone did it, right? You already said you can't think of anything out of the ordinary that happened to cause this."

"I know, but… Mom would never curse me. I'm sure of

it." She'd said the words, but there was no conviction in her tone.

"Char," I said.

She closed her eyes. "I know, Marion. I. Know. I just can't wrap my head around how a mother could curse her own daughter." Anger flashed bright in her eyes. "There has to be some thread of evil lurking inside of a person to do something like that. I know our relationships with her are complicated, I just never imagined that they'd be *this* complicated."

"I know." We sat in silence for a long time, picking at the pie. I placed mine on the coffee table. "I'm not hungry anymore."

"Me either." Charlotte stood, picked up my plate, and took them both to the kitchen.

I glanced at the clock. It was well past ten in the evening, and for the first time all night I thought of Jax. Hadn't he said he'd call me? After fishing my phone out of my pocket, I checked my messages. Nothing.

That was very strange. Even though we hadn't made any plans, it was unusual for us to spend the night apart. And when we did, we always talked before bed. A tiny thread of worry took up residence in my gut. It wasn't like Jax to not even call, especially after he'd said he would.

I quickly scrolled through my contacts and then hit his number. The call immediately went to voice mail, indicating either his phone was dead or it was turned off. "Jax, it's Marion. Call me when you get this. Today has been one for the books."

Charlotte reappeared and raised a curious eyebrow. "No hot contractor tonight?"

"I guess not." I didn't tell her that he wouldn't come over because of her dog. After bonding with her earlier, I didn't want to ruin that by bringing up something that might make her feel bad.

"That's too bad." She gave me a cheeky grin. "I have to admit that running into him in the middle of the night was the highlight of my week. Damn, Marion. For an old guy, he's droolworthy."

"He's not old," I insisted. "And yes, I agree. He's very handsome."

"Not old. Sure, just keep telling yourself that. Before you know it, AARP is going to come calling, and you'll be outside yelling at people to get off your lawn." She snickered, and even though she was needling me about my age, I didn't care. I liked this Charlotte. The playful one who was all smiles and fun to be around.

"What are you talking about?" I asked. "I'm already getting mail from AARP, and just last week I yelled at some kids for riding their bikes through my flower bed."

"Not through the tulips!" she said, sounding horrified. "They deserved flat tires and butt sores."

I let out a guffaw. "You can say that again."

A quiet lull fell over us, and after a moment, I said, "I think we should test what our magic can do."

She blinked at me. "What?"

"I'm fairly certain the answer to breaking your curse is for us to combine our magic. If that's the case, I think we should explore it. Then once we're comfortable, we can scout out the people who were at Hallucinations the night you got into town so we can cure them of their ailments. Maybe even find your ex and reverse that compulsion spell you cast on him."

"That's..." She shook her head. Then she closed her eyes and covered her face with her hands. Finally she muttered, "What if I end up cursing you?"

"Obviously, I can't say that it won't happen, but I'm willing to take the chance."

She emerged from behind her hands. "Why?"

"Because I was there when we cured Bradley. I know what that felt like, and I really just don't think it's going to happen. After what Hecate said—"

"That was really vague, Marion," she insisted.

"It wasn't that vague. And this just feels right to me. I trust you. Can you trust me?"

"Dammit." Charlotte gritted her teeth and then finally stood. "Fine. Let's do this, but I want it noted that I am skeptical and can't promise you won't end up with a wart on your nose."

"I'm pretty sure Lance has a procedure that can help with the wart. But this might make you feel better about the entire thing." I reached into my bag and pulled out the dagger that had chosen me only weeks earlier. With my hand wrapped around the hilt, the blade shimmered blue and a thread of magic pulsed up my arm.

"What exactly are you going to do with that? Stab me in the heart if my curse gives you the female version of ED?"

"Female version of ED? What exactly is that? A lack of sex drive? I promise you, there is no chance of that. Not

106

with the hot contractor boyfriend hanging around. But either way, I promise not to stab you. This is just to help me control my magic. I've been told it makes me more powerful. If you try to curse me, I'll ward it off with this."

"I'm not sure about this, Marion."

"I know, but you're going to do it anyway, right?"

"I guess."

"Good. Now come over here." I pointed to the spot beside me in the middle of the living room.

She did as I asked and then frowned. "Now what? Do you just want me to try to spell you or something?"

"No. You're going to spell something else, and then together we're going to reverse it."

Minx jumped up from the couch and hightailed it to the guestroom.

I laughed.

"Smart dog," Charlotte said.

"Definitely." I glanced around the room, looking for something that we could use to practice our skills on. There. The wooden owl clock that I'd picked up at a rummage sale a few months ago. I turned and pointed at it. "Do you think you can spell the clock to do something? Like make the owl's eye's move?"

"I can try, but I hope you're not attached to that ugly thing. Seriously, Marion, what possessed you to buy that? I think it deserves to be cursed."

She had a point. The owl was standing on a surf board and was wearing a shirt that read *If it swells, ride it.* "It made me laugh."

"Old people are weird," she said with a smirk.

"Guilty. Now do your thing." I took a step back and waited as she thought for a moment.

It wasn't long before she walked over to the clock, touched the owl's head and said, "Watch over my sister. Keep an eye out for bad actors." Magic flashed from her fingertips, lit up the clock, and then quickly blinked out.

Charlotte stepped back, taking a place beside me. We both peered at the clock.

"It doesn't look like—"

Before I could get my sentence out, the clock began to shake violently. And for a brief moment, I thought the entire thing was just going to come apart. But then the shaking stopped and the owl's eyes began to vibrate.

"Holy crap, this is weird," Charlotte said.

"Weird, but also fascinating, don't you think?"

She gave me a what-the-fuck look before turning her attention back to the possessed bird. The vibrating stopped, and one eye popped completely out of its head and then fixated on Charlotte. The other eye roamed around, appearing to take in the entire room over and over and over again.

"Good goddess, that's creepy," Charlotte said, moving to stand behind me. The eye followed her every movement.

"Very," I agreed.

"Marion!" Charlotte exclaimed as she moved to the other side of me. "Look at it! That thing is going to be watching me for the rest of my life. I'm never going to be able to leave my room again."

That would solve Jax's problem, I thought, but kept it to myself. The owl really was fixated on my sister, and even I had to admit that it was enough to give a person nightmares for the rest of their days. "Okay, let's put it out of its misery."

"How are we going to do that?" she asked.

"We're going to will it to stop creeping on us. With our combined magic."

She snorted. "I don't know why you think you need me to do that. Why don't you just wield that dagger and see what happens?"

"Well, my hunch is that we need each other to break any curses, but if you want me to try first, then okay." I tightened my grip on my dagger and walked over to the clock. The protruding eye stayed focused on my sister, while the other swirled faster and faster the closer I got to it.

I averted my gaze, trying to ward off the sudden nausea. "That thing is gonna make me vomit."

"It was vomit worthy before I cast that spell," Charlotte said, making me laugh.

I shook my head. "How did I ever get along without you?" I asked.

"You clearly didn't if you were decorating with that trash."

"It's funny," I insisted.

"If you say so." There was humor in her tone, and even though we were dealing with a serious problem, I felt even lighter than I had since I'd moved to Premonition Pointe. Like maybe my sister had been the final piece in the life I was building in my new home.

"Better get on with it," she said. "Or else I'm going to obliterate it. Being watched like that is really disturbing."

"Okay, calm down. Let me see what I can do." It wasn't every day that I tried to use magic. I hadn't even had the dagger all that long. In the past, I'd only used my newfound power when it was a life-or-death situation, so summoning my magic was sort of foreign.

Taking a deep breath, I gripped the dagger, felt the magic surge up my arm, and then focused on the clock. Instead of making a command, I envisioned the owl in his original form. My power crawled from my fingers, still wrapped around the dagger, up that arm and down the other. As I reached out to the clock, the magic burst from my palm, coating the owl. It burned bright, sparking with energy. The owl suddenly righted itself, its eyes back where they belonged.

"See, I told you it probably didn't have anything to do with me," Charlotte said.

I lowered my arm, but as soon as I did, the owl returned to its creepy form, one eye tracking me and the other focused on Charlotte.

"Oh, hell. It's possessed," Charlotte said. "If we throw it out, is it going to come back to haunt us? It's going to show up in my bed, isn't it?"

"Oh, hell no. We're not letting that happen." I dropped the dagger and grabbed my sister's hand. Together, we touched the clock face. Magic swirled around it, coating it just like it had coated Bradley's face. Everything popped back into place on the clock, and before we even moved our hands away, the magic disappeared. Confident our job was done, I dropped Charlotte's hand.

We stood together, watching the clock tick for a full minute before she turned to me and said, "I'll be damned."

"Looks like you were right when you said we were a team." I grinned at her. "Tomorrow we start tracking down the victims from Hallucinations."

CHAPTER 12

*T*he air was heavily saturated with fog when I turned onto Jax's street the next morning. It was still early, just after seven. I'd woken to a text from Jax with an apology for not getting in touch earlier. He'd had a full day at work and then got home and immediately went to work on the water heater.

Instead of returning the text, I quickly got dressed, ran by the coffee shop, and headed to his house unannounced. Thankful to find his truck still parked in the driveway, I pulled in beside him and quietly let myself in the front door.

His bed was rumpled but empty, and once again, I heard the rush of water in the pipes. With his coffee cup in hand, I slipped into the bathroom and grinned when I caught a sweet view of his backside through the clear glass door.

Damn, that man was sexy.

He turned at that exact moment, saw me standing there, and crooked his finger.

I put the coffee down and pulled my clothes off. When I opened the shower door, he pulled me in and pinned me against the wall.

With his lips already on my neck, he said, "I was just thinking about you."

"Is that right?"

He glanced down at his naked body, his gaze lingering on his hard shaft.

"I see. I guess I need to do something about that." I turned us so that he was against the tile and with the hot water sluicing over us, I kissed my way down his neck, his pecs, and took my time tasting his abs until I kneeled down, wrapped my hand around him, and opened my mouth.

Jax didn't hesitate to slide into my waiting mouth. At the first taste of him, I let out a tiny moan that he echoed.

"Holy hell, Marion," he said, sliding his hands into my hair. "I can never get enough of you."

His words made my chest swell with pride and desire that spurred me on to take him deeper until his cock hit the back of my throat.

"Fuck," he muttered as he stared down at me, pure lust burning from his dark gaze.

I kept my eyes on his as I worked him over, reveling in how much I turned him on. It was a power I'd never known with anyone else. The fire that burned between us seemed to only get more intense as time went on, and I was starting to believe that it would never extinguish. After all the years of wanting and needing him, my fears were finally starting to settle.

"I'm not going to last if you keep that up," he said with a growl.

I smiled around him and redoubled my efforts, wanting nothing more than to bring him pleasure.

"Marion," he said as he pulled away, leaving my mouth feeling empty.

I pouted up at him.

"Don't worry, baby. I'm putting that mouth back to work right now." He reached down and lifted me up. My legs went around him automatically as he steadied me against the wall, claiming my mouth with a rough kiss while simultaneously slamming into me.

My head swam as I was overwhelmed by his complete possession of my mind and body. There was nothing like being taken by him, this man I craved. The one I trusted completely. The one who made me feel like the sexiest woman alive.

Jax thrust into me, over and over again, his hands on my ass, digging into my flesh. Then he shifted slightly and found just the right spot.

My entire body tensed as spasm after spasm rolled through me. I clung to him, riding out my pleasure as he took his. Finally, he slammed into me one last time, bit down on my shoulder, and emptied himself inside of me.

Jax held me there, his head buried in my shoulder as I ran my hands down his back. It was always in this quiet moment, right after, while we were recovering from our lovemaking, when I felt the closest to him. Both of us vulnerable, our bodies and emotions both naked. There were no barriers in those precious few minutes.

"Jesus, Marion. I love you more than you know," he said, feathering light kisses up my neck.

"I love you, too," I said with a contented sigh. "I missed you the last two nights."

He chuckled softly. "I think it's obvious that I missed you, too." His lips lingered briefly on my own before he kissed me one last time and then reluctantly pulled away from me. "If I don't stop touching you, I'm going to be very late for my meeting."

I ran two fingers down the middle of his chest, just to see what he would do.

He grabbed my hand, stopping me. "You're trying to kill me, aren't you?"

"Just torture you a little."

"It's working." He turned his back to me, quickly washed off, and then exited the shower. "Take as long as you want. I'm going to jump in some clothes and head out."

"There's coffee on the counter," I called as I ducked my head under the spray.

"Found it."

When I emerged ten minutes later, my sex god was gone and all that was left was a note that said, *See you tonight?*

I answered with one word. *Yes.*

I WAS on my way back to my house when a call came in from the Liminal Day Spa.

"Marion?" Lance said. "We've got another Hallucinations client with a terrible case of acne. He heard from Bradley that this was the place to come to find the cure. Can you and your sister make time to check him out today?"

"We should be able to." I glanced at the clock on my dash. "Give us about twenty-five to thirty minutes."

"I'm sure Denver will be here. He seems quite desperate. He said something about his boyfriend leaving him if he didn't get his issues worked out. I assume that means he has a sagging flagpole as well."

"Sagging flagpole? Seriously, Lance?" I asked with a chuckle.

"I'm at the front desk with customers waiting. What else am I supposed to call it?"

"Flagpole it is then."

I was still laughing when I called Charlotte to let her know I was on my way to pick her up, but that all changed when I pulled up to my house and spotted the woman on my front porch.

Liana Adler, the mother whom I hadn't spoken to in years, was wearing an oversized sweater that was hanging off one shoulder and a white cotton skirt with strappy sandals, and her long strawberry-blond hair flowed in waves down her back. Her petite frame was so much smaller than either me or Charlotte, it was hard to not think of her as fairy-like. She'd always been beautiful and charming, two traits that got her out of a lot of sticky situations over the years. But not this time. Not here. Not with me. When I saw her, all I could think of was her packing up and leaving an eight-year-old behind with a family she barely knew.

"Marion," my mother cried the moment I stepped out of

my SUV. "I tried to call, but all I got was voice mail. I'm sorry to just show up like this, but—"

I held up my hand, stopping her. "I don't know why you're here so early without an invitation, but Charlotte and I are in a hurry. So whatever this is about, it'll have to wait." I stormed past her into the house and was met by a very frantic Minx, who was barking and growling at the door. There were tiny scratches on the doorframe, indicating she'd been trying to claw her way out.

"It's okay, Minx. She's not coming in," I said, picking her up just as the door swung open and Liana Adler strode in as if she owned the place.

Minx tore out of my grip and launched herself at my mother.

"Marion Matched! Get this dog off me!" she cried as Minx sank her teeth into her sweater and started to pull on it.

"Minx!" Charlotte barked. "Come here."

The dog instantly let go of our mother and hurried over to Charlotte's feet. My sister picked her up and cuddled her against her chest.

"That dog needs a muzzle," Liana said, sounding disgusted as she smoothed her sweater.

"She was only doing what she's supposed to do," I said.

"What's that? Terrorize your guests?" Liana glared at the dog, clearly disgusted.

"No, protect the house from intruders," I said flatly.

My mother stared at me as her eyes narrowed. "I am your mother, Marion Marie. I didn't raise you to speak to me like that."

Everything inside of me tensed, and I suddenly felt like I was going to explode. With my teeth clenched and my body shaking with anger, I said, "Let me remind you, *Mother*, that you did very *little* to raise me. Even before you left the first time, you left that job to Dad. You're going to have to leave now. Charlotte and I are on our way out."

Liana's shoulders slumped as all the fight seemed to drain out of her. She shook her head slowly. "I'm sorry, Marion. This isn't how I envisioned our reunion going. Can you give me just a few minutes before you rush off?"

"No, Mom," Charlotte said softly. "We have an appointment, and it can't wait." My sister met my gaze as she added, "But maybe we can meet somewhere for lunch?"

It was right there on the tip of my tongue to say that we couldn't. That we had to work. Or that we'd planned to go alien hunting. Anything so that I wouldn't have to repeat this awful moment in just a few short hours. But my mother chimed in before I could make our excuses.

"Can it be somewhere private? I have something important to share, and I just wouldn't be comfortable at a restaurant."

Against my better judgment, I said, "What is it?"

She swallowed hard as she met Charlotte's eyes. "I missed you, baby."

"Mom, we can't do this right now," Charlotte said. "If you want to talk to us, meet us at Bird's Eye Café at one o'clock." She pointed to the door. "Now go. If you stay here, Minx will finish tearing apart that sweater."

Liana glanced at me, her eyes pleading as if she wanted me to override my sister. I just shrugged. "She's right. As soon as Charlotte and I leave, Minx will be out for blood again."

"Fine. If that's what you two want," Liana said. "I'll meet you at Bird's Eye Café in a few hours. But I don't know what's wrong with meeting back here."

Neither of us answered her.

Liana Adler sighed dramatically and then spun on her heel and walked out my front door.

I gave my sister an appreciative nod. "Impressive. Can we come up with a secret signal so you can make her disappear like that at lunch when I can't take even one more moment of her passive-aggressive behavior?"

Charlotte snorted. "Believe me when I say I'm certain *I'll* break before you do. Come on. I need something to cheer me up. Let's go cure some acne and get that man's penis working again."

CHAPTER 13

"*I*s this going to hurt?" Denver asked as he covered his crotch with both hands.

"Not unless you want one of us to kick you in the balls." Charlotte smiled sweetly at the tall, thin man in the wire-rimmed glasses.

"Um, I think I'll pass on that treatment," he said with a grimace.

"Good plan." Charlotte winked. "I'm sure your girlfriend wouldn't like it either."

"Ha. Well, since I don't have one of those, nor a wife, that's the least of my concerns."

"My condolences." Charlotte grinned at him and he grinned back.

What in the world was going on here? Was Charlotte really flirting with the man on the procedure table?

Lance, who was standing behind us, shook his head and chuckled. "This world is a crazy place. I'll be up at the front desk. Denver, Laura will be in to get started on that massage after these ladies are done."

"Thanks." The man nodded to Lance. "My hamstrings will be forever grateful."

The door shut quietly behind Lance, leaving me and Charlotte with the acne-stricken man. His breakout was so severe, it was almost painful to even look at him.

"I'm so sorry about this," Charlotte said, moving closer to him.

"Why?" Worry flickered in his bright blue eyes. "I thought you said this wasn't going to hurt?"

"It's not," I interjected quickly. "Or at least it shouldn't. She's just sorry you've had to deal with this."

"She's not the only one," he said with a grimace. "I honestly thought I was having an allergic reaction to something. I've never had a breakout even remotely like this. Not even as a teenager. But Lance said it happens sometimes. Something about hormonal imbalances or not eating enough superfoods. He said my body might be fighting back after a weekend of debauchery and overindulgence."

Charlotte raised one eyebrow. "What did you do? Have a weekend in Vegas that you can't quite remember?"

He laughed. "Something like that. Though it was here in Premonition Pointe, and it involved a lot of margaritas and way too many fresh donuts from the Bird's Eye Café."

"That sounds like Sunday brunch to me," I said with a snicker.

He laughed, too, and I found myself liking this man. Here he was, covered in acne that looked like something out of a horror film, and instead of being embarrassed or stressed about it, he was joking around and even flirting with my sister. Any man who was that secure in himself might be worth her time. And, bonus, he was single.

"Let's get this taken care of," I said, moving to take my place next to Charlotte. I could feel the nervous energy radiating off her, but I doubted Denver could sense her trepidation. I knew she was just worried about the magic backfiring again, but to her credit, she had a smile on her face and was watching me, waiting for me to get the healing started.

"What does this healing look like?" Denver asked. "A cream? A potion? A human sacrifice?"

"Human sacrifice?" Charlotte exclaimed, her eyes wide with shock. "What kind of witches do you think we are?" When his eyes crinkled at the corners with amusement, she gave him a flat stare and shook her head. "Ha, ha. Very funny. All you need to do is sit there and look pretty. We'll do the rest."

He groaned. "I'm doomed to look like this forever then."

I rolled my eyes. "If you two are done, maybe we can get on with it?"

"Sure, Miss Marion. I'm ready. Change me from a frog to a Prince Charming, then maybe Charlotte here won't laugh in my face when I ask her out."

Charlotte's face flushed.

All I could do was grin. It was one of those instances when I didn't need to see anyone's aura to know that these two had a lot of potential. I just hoped for Charlotte's sake that the magic we were about to unleash did the trick to erase the curse she'd given him, or eventually they were going to have one heck of an uncomfortable conversation when he found out she was responsible.

"Just relax, Denver. Charlotte and I have this covered." I grabbed my sister's hand and asked her, "Ready?"

When she nodded, we each used our other hands to press them to his cheeks. The magic was once again immediate as it washed over his face and moved down his neck toward the rest of his body.

Denver closed his startling blue eyes and seemed to revel in the magic, soaking it up, letting it heal every part of him. And just like before, as quickly as the magic appeared, it vanished, leaving one stunning man in its wake.

"Whoa," Charlotte and I said at the same time.

Denver grinned at us. "Is that a good thing?"

"Oh, it's a very good thing," she agreed, gazing at him like she couldn't tear her eyes away. Who could blame her? The man had a face that was meant for the big screen.

But his looks weren't why I was stunned when the magic vanished. It was because their auras were so perfectly matched, the deep violet colors melding into each other as if they'd been loving partners for years.

This man was Charlotte's perfect match. There was no doubt about it.

Both of them looked at me.

"Marion?" My sister nudged me. "Snap out of your trance. You're practically married, remember?"

Married? Jax and I hadn't even discussed marriage. But that was hardly the point. Charlotte thought I was lusting after the man we'd just cured. I chuckled to myself. "Sorry. I was just thinking that you should invite Denver to our mixer on Thursday."

"Mixer?" Denver asked, looking interested. "For what? A charity or something?"

"No," Charlotte said, her face flushing again. "My sister is a matchmaker and is hosting a mixer for a couple of new clients. She wants to add you to the guest list."

"Will you be there?" he asked her.

Charlotte smiled at him. "I'm one of the clients."

"Then I'll be there." He grabbed her hand and held it for a long moment. "It was really nice to meet you, Charlotte."

"You, too, Denver."

"WELL, that certainly makes my job easy," I said on our way out of the spa. "Though I suppose I'm gonna need to find another bachelorette for all the men I invited to come meet you at the mixer."

"Hmm?" Charlotte asked distractedly with a moony look on her face.

"Good goddess," I said, laughing. "You just met the man, and you're already head over heels."

"Can you blame me? Did you see those eyes? And his sense of humor." She let out a contented sigh. "No man in the history of ever has been that confident while being covered in zits. That's not the type of man who is going to lose his shit when his girl has a male friend or when she finds her own success. That's the type of man who knows who he is and isn't afraid to be real. Do you know what I mean?"

"Sure," I said as we slid into my SUV. "But I think you might be making a lot of assumptions based on one first impression. Maybe dial it back just a touch until you get to know him a little?" I suggested.

"Oh, I know." She waved a hand, dismissing my concerns. "I just meant that's what he was laying down. And if that proves to be accurate, I'm picking it up every single time."

"Can't argue with that. Here's to the mixer tomorrow night. May the love gods be with all of us. Not that you have anything to worry about. The aura match you two have is off the charts."

She gave me an easy smile. "I thought that's what the deep purple meant. But I wouldn't mind a little of that red fire you and Jax have."

I snorted. "Judging by the flirting you two had going on, I'm guessing that's not going to be a problem."

"I sure hope you're right. It's been way too long since I've had a big O, or even a little one. Eli wasn't very skilled at finding the *right spot* if you get my drift."

"Is it time for Charlotte to get her groove back?" I teased.

"It's way past time. Like dusty cobwebs past time. I just hope I don't jump him in the bathroom at the mixer. It could be a little embarrassing if your business partner was overheard in one of the stalls, getting it on with one of the guests."

"Probably better to wait." I nodded sagely. "We definitely

wouldn't want my *business partner* tarnishing the agency's reputation."

She snickered. "I knew you'd catch that."

"Let's just start with magical partners first and see where things go," I suggested.

Charlotte eyed me and nodded. "Fair enough."

There was silence in the SUV as I pulled into a parking space in the Bird's Eye Café parking lot. We were a little bit early for the meeting with our mother, so I turned to my sister and said, "Now that we know our magic definitely works on those you cursed, we need to come up with a game plan to find the rest of those poor men who were at Hallucinations that night."

"Okay. What do you suggest?" The trepidation she'd had earlier about using her magic seemed to be gone, and for that I was grateful.

"Lance already knows to call us. Since we don't want to advertise that you accidentally cursed them, I was thinking of telling Skyler down at Sky's the Limit to keep an eye out. Plus we can ask the coven members to be on alert, too. Hope's husband has a furniture store, and she's a party planner. She can also hear thoughts sometimes, so that would be helpful. Grace is a Realtor and sees a lot of people. The others don't do a lot with the public, but I'm sure they can keep an ear open when they are around town. I'll also tell Ty and Kennedy. The one I'm worried about is Damon Grant. If Carly can't get us in to see him, we'll never get near him."

She bit down on her bottom lip. "Damon Grant. Yeah.

Let's hope Carly has some sway, or that poor man's career might be over."

"That would be tragic."

"Very."

I quickly made a few phone calls to the coven and Skyler's shop to tell them we were ready to start the healing, and then we both reluctantly made our way into the Bird's Eye Café to find out why our mother was in town.

CHAPTER 14

"Maybe she couldn't find it?" Charlotte said as we both stared at the front doors of Bird's Eye Café.

"How could she not find it?" I asked, exasperated. "It's right on the main highway that goes through town. It's not like it's tucked back into the woods or anything."

My sister shrugged one shoulder. "I don't know. I guess I was trying to give her the benefit of the doubt."

I scoffed, well past my tolerance for being charitable to Liana Adler. "She's an hour late, Charlotte. And she's not answering your calls or texts. I think it's safe to say this is just her trying to punish us for not doing exactly what she wanted when she wanted us to do it."

Charlotte closed her eyes and took a deep breath. "I know. It's totally her MO. I guess I just keep hoping that one of these days she'll break that cycle."

I raised both eyebrows. "We're talking about a woman

who chooses herself over her children every time, Char. Every single time. Whatever she wanted to tell us, she's keeping it to herself now because we hurt her feelings when we didn't drop our plans and hear her out." I gentled my voice when I added, "You do realize that, right?"

"I do. Of course I do." She sounded angry now. "She's been manipulating me my entire life. I didn't go no contact with her because of the fireman at the dog park. That's just a dumb story I use so I don't have to explain anything or talk about it. The real reason is that she blindsided me and took me to meet my bio dad by telling me we were going to see my father. No other information. Just, 'We're meeting your father for dinner.' I thought she meant Memphis. I knew they talked occasionally, so I didn't think anything of it and was happy to go see him."

My stomach started to ache on her behalf. "She took you to meet Arlo Ray?"

She nodded, her jaw tight. "On a yacht."

I blinked at her. "What? You can't be serious."

"Oh, I'm serious," she said with a huff. "I knew as soon as we got there that something was off. Pops would never rent a yacht or even sign up for a dinner cruise. That's not even remotely his thing. But she insisted and we were there, so I got on that damned boat."

My heart ached for her. Forcing Charlotte to meet her biological father for the first time without a way to exit was by far the worst thing she'd ever done besides leaving us. "I'm sorry, Char. What happened?"

"The next thing I knew, we were headed out to sea. And I was stuck there with the two of them acting like we were some kind of tightknit happy family. He wanted to know everything about me, what I was up to, what my future plans were, and he wanted to make plans to do more things together. All I wanted to do was punch him in the face and walk off. It was all so surreal and unbelievable. What is it with those two, thinking just because I share biology with that man, that I want to have anything to do with him? He was never there for me. He walked out before I was even born. And now that I'm a fully grown adult, he wants a relationship? Hell no. Fuck him. Fuck her too for putting me in that position." Charlotte stood abruptly. "I'm done waiting. Can we go home now?"

"Absolutely." I threw some money down on the table for the waitress, even though we hadn't ordered anything but water, and followed my sister out of the restaurant.

We were almost back to my house when my phone rang. I accepted the call on my car's Bluetooth.

It was Skyler. "I have a live one for you. Poor guy was ready to buy out the entire skincare line in order to try to clear up his skin. I also overheard him tell someone on his cell phone that he was looking into penis pumps. So if you hurry, you might save him a few bucks."

I glanced at Charlotte. "Are you up for another round of healing?"

"Absolutely. We're on our way, Skyler," she said. "Give us ten minutes. Do you think he'll stick around?"

"If I tell him a cure is coming and I can save him hundreds? Definitely."

∼

"So how many men have had their love sticks restored?" Celia asked me the next afternoon.

"Six? No seven, including Bradley, the first guy we met at the spa," I said as I admired the flower arrangements Gigi had provided for the mixer. We'd had a last minute venue change when the owner of the bookstore called to tell me the store was having electrical and plumbing issues and they were going to have to close for a week or so. In a panic, I immediately called Hope to try and help us get it moved. She'd worked all her contacts, but with it being so last minute, no one could help. That's when Gigi stepped in and said we could use her house.

Gigi and her fiancé, Sebastian, lived in a large house overlooking the Pacific Ocean. Her living room was spacious, but what made it spectacular was her large patio that was perfect for parties. We'd decorated the outside with twinkle lights, and there were flowers everywhere from Tazia's nursery.

"Damon is refusing to see anyone," Celia reported. "I swear, what a man-baby. If I hear him say one more time that his career is over, I'm going to vomit. It's not like he's dead. Like some of us."

"I'm sure he's upset that the acne isn't clearing up. It probably doesn't help that he has to stay off that ankle for a number of weeks, too," I said, sympathizing with the guy. His movie was about to be canceled, and there wasn't anything he could do about it. Or at least, he didn't *realize* there was something he could do about it, because even though they'd tried several times, he wouldn't see Carly or

Joy. Neither of them had the opportunity to tell him there was a cure for at least part of his problems.

"There's being upset, and then there's being petulant," the ghost said, sounding disgusted. "He'd be better served to be like Petey Lemongrass. Now there's a man who is ready to take the world by the balls."

"Petey Lemongrass?" I asked as I uncorked a bottle of red wine. Our mixer was smaller than normal, so we hadn't hired a bartender.

"Oh, yeah. Real hunky dude that runs a fishing boat out of the marina. He's been out there every day, doing his job diligently. Not hiding at home so no one will see his acne-marred skin. You just gotta admire that, you know?"

I paused to stare at my ghost. "You know of a man Charlotte cursed, and you're just now telling me?"

"I've been busy! Do you know how much work it is keeping an eye on that pretty boy?"

I closed my eyes and prayed for patience. "Celia, you do realize you don't need to watch Damon twenty-four-seven, right?"

"Of course I do. How else do you think I know about Petey?"

I crossed my arms over my chest. "Okay. Who else in town needs me and Charlotte to pay them a visit?"

"Hmm, let's see. Lenny Kips, Billie Fitts, and Wilson Quincy."

"Okay, and where do I find these people?" I asked.

"Hallucinations. They all work there. I can't believe you didn't think to go by there. That one was obvious." Celia shook her head at me. "Have you just been spending too much time with your hunky contractor? I know how it is when you're too sexed up. The brain sort of stops working."

I rolled my eyes, but mostly to cover up the fact that I hadn't actually seen much of Jax lately due to his busy schedule and the fact that he was keeping his distance because of Minx. He was, however, supposed to join us at the mixer later. "I'll put them on the list. Hopefully, Charlotte and I can stop there on the way home tonight."

"Stop where?" Charlotte asked, stepping up beside me.

I filled her in on Celia's information. "We have some more people to help."

"Uh, tonight?"

"Yeah. Is that a problem?" I asked, getting a little irritated. I'd spent most of the week with her, tracking down victims of her curse, and here she was, reluctant to do what we both knew needed to be done.

"No, it's just that Denver and I were planning to go for a midnight stroll on the beach after the mixer. It's supposed to be recharging. That's what Denver says anyway."

"And who is watching Minx while you're out at all hours ?" I asked, already knowing the answer.

She gave me a pleading look. "It's just one night. And Minx loves you. You don't really mind, do you?"

The truth was I didn't have any problem at all watching her dog. But Minx had a problem with Jax, and I didn't want to spend the night trying to keep her from chewing his foot off. "Charlotte. What about Jax?"

"She's never going to get used to him if he keeps avoiding her. I swear, she'll calm down," she said, though she sounded a little doubtful.

"Ugh. Fine. Go. Have fun with your new man, but if she draws blood, we're gonna have words. And we need to stop by Hallucinations first. Those guys deserve to be released from the curse." Why did I so often feel like the mom in our relationship? Probably because our own mother had skipped out for so many years. We still hadn't even heard from her since she stood us up the day before.

"You're the best." Charlotte gave me a quick hug and then went off to greet the guests that were starting to arrive.

I went to check the patio one last time and found Gigi and Sebastian leaning against the railing, staring out at the moonlit night.

"Marion," Gigi said, her eyes bright. "You made my home look fabulous. I can't wait for the love connections to start happening."

"Me? Your place is the definition of gorgeous. I just tried not to mess anything up."

"I like the lights," Sebastian said. "Do you think we can keep those?"

Gigi laughed. "Really?" she asked him. "I think we can put up our own lights if you're that into them."

"You can keep them. Consider them payment for doing me this huge favor," I said.

"Anything for my new coven sister." Gigi gave me a quick hug. "Now go on. There's an incredibly handsome man standing by the back door who looks like he might need your attention."

I turned and spotted Jax wearing a pair of clean jeans and a formfitting black button-down shirt. His hair had been styled in what I'd started referring to as a hero cut.

The sides were cut neatly with the top longer and styled with just enough product to give it some body. I swear, he looked like he'd just walked off the pages of *GQ*.

"Hey, you," I said, slipping my arms around his waist. "You're smokin' hot. Make sure you stick with me so our bachelorette of the evening doesn't get any ideas."

His eyes danced with humor. "You mean the one who just told me I'm way too old for her?"

"She did not," I said, exaggerating the shock in my tone. "How dare she."

He chuckled. "She might be right, though. I've had my sights on someone just a little more mature than a twenty-six-year-old." He dipped his head and gave me a long lingering kiss. When he pulled back, he smiled lazily at me. "That's better."

I would've loved to stand there and make out with him all night, but I had a job to do. There were two clients who needed me to help them find their love matches. Riley, my guy who was looking for a same-sex partner, was going to be easy. He'd turned out to be a personable guy who seemed at ease with everyone he met. But Jana? My twenty-six-year-old pastry chef couldn't find two words to string together even if they were in one of her recipe books. Since she was up at 4:00 a.m. most days to get her baking done, she'd been suffering from lack of conversation and it showed. Small talk was going to be her downfall. Even if she did find an aura connection, I still needed her to find a way to communicate with her potential dates.

"I need to get back in there," I told Jax. "But feel free to stay out here and talk to Gigi and Sebastian if you want to.

I'll come find you when I get a break." I pressed up on my tiptoes and kissed his cheek. "If I forget later, thanks for coming tonight. It makes me feel better knowing your close by."

"Always," he said and brushed his thumb over my cheek. I leaned in to him, wishing we could stay like that forever, but then quickly pulled away and slipped back inside. I knew if I didn't go then, I would never leave the patio.

"You are so lucky," Jana said, pressing her hand to her heart. "Your boyfriend is perfect."

I gave her an indulgent smile. "No one is perfect. But I do agree with you that I'm lucky. And you will be too. Come on. Let's get you mingling."

The petite brunette, with blue eyes so deep they were almost violet, looked like someone had stolen her favorite puppy. "Mingle?"

"Yes. I'm going to introduce you to some of the men who came to get to know you."

She swallowed hard but nodded and followed me to the circle of men I'd recruited for Charlotte before she'd met Denver. They all turned to us as we approached, each of them eyeing Jana with interest.

Jana took a step forward with her hand out. "I'm Jana. I —oomph!" She tripped on what appeared to be nothing and plowed right into David, the man who owned the Premonition Pointe dog hotel. He'd taken over from his parents when they'd retired and moved to Santa Barbara.

"Whoa," he said, catching her. "Are you all right?"

Jana seemed to have swallowed her tongue as she worked her mouth but didn't get anything out.

Goddess above. This was one of the reasons I'd opened my dating agency to help women and men over forty find their love matches. The only reason I took on Jana was so that all the men who'd been invited for Charlotte would have a chance at meeting someone age-appropriate. People over forty were so much more confident in who they were and knew exactly what they were looking for. The younger ones could sometimes be disasters just due to pure nerves. I was certain that was Jana's issue. I just needed to get her out of her head.

"Jana, this is David. He owns a dog hotel. David, this is Jana. She's a pastry chef at Blueberries."

"Dog hotel?" Jana asked at the same time David said, "Pastry Chef? I think I'm in love already."

Jana chuckled and placed a soft hand on his chest as she said, "You could have been a little more original, but I'll take that over 'Oh, I could never date a pastry chef because I'd never lose this holiday weight.'"

"Tell me a man didn't say that to you," David said.

"No can do. The last man I went on a date with got up in the middle of dinner and left when I told him I had eclairs in my fridge for dessert if he was so inclined. He didn't even pay the bill. He just… left."

"Loser," David said.

A few more of the men in the area commented on her experience, and by the time I stepped away to find Charlotte, Jana's eyes were lit with happiness and she was busy engaging in conversation with six different men. If that's all it took to get her talking, then maybe not all hope of finding her someone special was lost.

I was making my way to the other side of the room when I spotted what looked like the back of my sister's head near the hallway that led to the off-limits area of the house. I put my hand up to wave at her, indicating it was time to get to work on reading auras, but was distracted when I heard a familiar voice behind me.

"Marion?" Brix said. "Do you have a minute?"

"Hey! You made it," I said, grinning up at him. But as soon as I saw the look on his face, my smile vanished. "Oh no. You heard, right?"

"Heard what?" he asked, his eyebrows pinching together as he scanned the ballroom, and his gaze landing in the direction where I'd last seen my sister.

"About Charlotte. I was going to tell you, but honestly, it just completely slipped my mind. There's been so much going on. I should have called."

"Marion," Brix growled. "Where is she?"

"Huh?" I frowned and glanced past him, scanning for my sister. "Well, she was just right over there." I nodded my head in her previous direction. "Only now I have no idea."

Brix grabbed my elbow and guided me toward where Charlotte had just been standing.

"Uh, want to tell me why you're manhandling me? It's not my fault Charlotte found someone before this mixer. And if you think this is going to make her decide you're better than Denver, then—"

"What are you talking about?" Brix asked between clenched teeth as his gaze continued to search for Charlotte.

"Charlotte and Denver. They met yesterday, and she

seems to think he's the one. Now you. What are you talking about?" I demanded.

"Holy hell, Marion. I thought you were telling me your sister was cursed with black magic."

"What? Why would you think that?" Was she? No way. I'd have felt it when we were doing our healing, wouldn't I? I prayed that was the case. Hecate had told us she was cursed to curse people, but I'd never in a million years have thought it was with black magic.

"You just said you were sorry you didn't tell me. I thought that's what you were talking about."

I shook my head. "I meant I was sorry I didn't tell you that Charlotte isn't the bachelorette for this shindig. I didn't want you to waste an evening chasing someone who has already been caught by someone else. I mean, already coupled up with someone else."

"Okay, consider me warned. Now, I need you to do something for me," Brix said.

I waited until he spoke again.

"Someone who is in this house right now is a black magic user. I need you to help me find them."

"Black magic?" I asked, my voice going high pitched. "That's impossible. I vet all my clients. No one here has a history of that." *Please let that be true. Please let that be true. Please let that be true.* I chanted it in my head over and over and over again.

"Vetted or not, it's happening." He held up a silver necklace that had a pentacle pendant. It was glowing. "This proves it." Brix moved the pendant right and then left and then right again. Every time he moved it toward the right, the pendant glowed brighter. "The black magic user is this way."

Brix strode off across the room, straight toward where my sister had been standing only a few moments earlier.

Fear rolled over me. Had Charlotte been cursed with black magic? Was Brix after her? He usually only worked high profile cases. Not one that involved a small time witch who'd accidentally cursed a bar full of men.

Without another thought, I rushed after Brix, determined to keep him away from Charlotte. No way was I letting him or anyone else lock her up for something she couldn't control. "Brix I think—"

"This way," he said and darted down the hallway. As soon as I caught up to him, I stopped in my tracks and watched as he kicked in one of the doors and rushed in, grabbing Charlotte and twisting her arms to her back. He slapped magical handcuffs on her and said, "You have the right to remain silent—"

"Marion? What's happening?" Charlotte asked, panic in her eyes.

I shook my head at her, not wanting her to say anything that could get her into more trouble.

"You're under arrest for using black magic," Brix told her.

"I'm not a black magic user," she insisted as she started to struggle against her restraints. "Tell him, Marion! Tell him how all of this is just a big misunderstanding. I never meant to hurt anyone!"

Brix stared her straight in the eye. "Stop talking. Right

now. I'm only telling you this because I respect and admire your sister, got me?"

She nodded, her eyes full of tears.

"Now move."

I watched, feeling completely helpless while Charlotte was frog-marched through the house, down the walkway, and then stuffed into the backseat of an SUV. As the taillights faded into the distance, I turned to my friends, found Sebastian, and said, "We need a lawyer ASAP."

"You got it." He nodded soberly. "I'll go right now and get her bailed out. Don't worry about a thing, Marion. I'll handle it, understood?"

"Understood," I said. But as I watched Sebastian leave the house, I couldn't shake the feeling that I wasn't going to see my sister for a very long time. A single tear fell down my cheek until I angrily wiped it away.

There was no time to break down. My sister needed me.

CHAPTER 15

"What happened?" Denver asked, sounding frantic as he approached with two glasses of wine in his hands. "Did I just see law enforcement take Charlotte away in cuffs?"

I nodded, not sure what to say. She'd only known this man for two days. Sure, she liked him, but that·didn't mean she wanted him filled in on her legal troubles.

"Why?" His jaw tensed as he started for the front door.

"I'm not really sure." It wasn't a total lie. I still couldn't wrap my head around the idea that Charlotte had somehow been using black magic. I just didn't believe it was possible. In spite of her accidental curses, she really didn't want to hurt people and wanted to make sure everyone affected was cured. She had a good heart and wasn't the type of person to inflict something as evil as black magic on anyone.

There had to be a mistake. A huge one.

"I overheard the agent say something about black magic," Jana said, staring up at Denver with heart eyes.

"Black magic?" he repeated, his face full of shock. "Are you sure?"

She nodded. "One hundred percent sure. I was two feet away when he cuffed her."

"Fuck." Denver slammed the wine glasses down on a side table and strode out of the house without looking back.

I winced. That was likely the last time Charlotte would see him. Surviving one accidental acne and ED curse was one thing, but hanging around someone who might turn your soul black was entirely another. I wanted to call him back or go after him to defend my sister, but what would I say? The Magical Task Force is wrong? She is too kind for that? She must've been framed?

It all sounded like bullshit even to my own ears.

"Marion," Jax said, grabbing my hand. "Come on. Let's go so we can be there when Sebastian gets Charlotte released. She's going to need you."

I clutched at his hand. "But the mixer. My clients. I can't just run off without at least saying something. And what about Gigi? I can't just leave her with this mess."

"Iris is taking over for you—" Jax started.

"And I've got this," Gigi said, cutting him off. "Go. Be there for Charlotte. That's what coven sisters are for. To hold each other up when we need it."

I grabbed her and hugged her hard. "Thank you. And tell Iris I couldn't do this job without her. She's a gem."

"She knows," Gigi said, waving us off. "Go. Don't worry about a thing here."

Jax nodded his thanks and then whisked me away into his truck. "We'll get your SUV later."

I waved a hand, not at all concerned. "Thank you. I think my head would've exploded if we'd stayed there while we waited for news."

"I know. That's why it's better to just go now. You won't rest until you know she's okay anyway."

He was right. I'd wear a hole in my hardwood floors waiting for that phone call. The only problem was Minx. She was home alone, and if someone didn't get to her soon, she'd be the one wearing holes in my furniture, my shoes, and anything else she could get her jaws around. I texted Ty, begging him to check on her and take her to his apartment if necessary.

Thankfully, he agreed without asking any questions.

What had I done to deserve such a wonderful young man in my life? I loved him like he was my own son. Kennedy, too. And I dreaded the day they moved out of my apartment and into their own home. Having them close was such a joy, not because they were there to watch Minx or help me with the home maintenance, but because I just loved having them around.

"What are you thinking about over there?" Jax asked me.

"Ty and Kennedy. I was just thinking how much I love having them around," I said as I stared blankly out the windshield.

There was a pregnant pause before Jax said, "She's going to be okay. You know that, right? She'll be back home with you in no time. Sebastian will make sure of it."

I closed my eyes, wishing I could just block out the

world. "I wish I believed that. I really do. But black magic, Jax? If they think she's been using it, they aren't even going to let us bail her out. She'll rot in a Magical Task Force holding cell until a trial." I clutched my hands into fists. "I just... I don't understand."

He reached over and grabbed my hand, squeezing it to show his report. "Whatever happens, I'll be by your side for all of it. And no matter what you need, I'm here to help."

"Even if it means I have to take in a chihuahua who hates your guts? Will I ever see you again if Minx is my permanent housemate?"

"Even then." He gave me a soft smile, making me almost lose my composure. This man had a heart of gold. I knew just how much of a nuisance Minx was when she was trying to eat his face off, yet here he was, offering to deal with her, no questions asked, because he knew I'd rather die than hand that dog off to someone else before Charlotte could get back home to care for her.

"I love you," I said.

His lips curved into a pleased smile. "I love you, too. Attack dog and all."

By the time we reached the Premonition Pointe law enforcement offices, my stomach was in knots. Nausea had taken over and my face was hot. Stress always did that to me.

All I could do was tell myself over and over again that Sebastian was the best. He'd handle it, and if he couldn't, he'd find someone who could. He'd built his business and reputation on being thorough and willing to do whatever it took to get the job done. We were lucky he was on our side.

"How long do you think it'll take?" I asked Jax.

"I have no idea. I've never been arrested."

"Never? Not once? Not even for mooning a cop while you went down the freeway?" A friend of his had once dared him to moon a cop, and when he did, the car he was riding in was pulled over and the cop had hauled him off to the station. He was seventeen at the time, and it had left an impression.

"I never said I hadn't taken a ride in a cop car, just that I've never been arrested. And that's true. The cop let me go if I promised to sign up to help at the bake sale that was happening the following weekend. I did, and I'll remind you that my table sold out first, despite the fact I'd baked twelve dozen cookies, three cakes, and three dozen cupcakes. It was a madhouse."

I shook my head at him. "You do realize they were there to support the hunky seventeen-year-old and not because your cupcakes rivaled something baked by Julia Childs, right?"

"Sure." He chuckled. "But it satisfied the cop and impressed my mom and my aunt... until they tasted the cookies. Turns out I used too much baking powder." He grimaced. "That was when I learned the value of read twice, measure once."

"Oh, I remember. I bought a dozen of those horrible cookies," I said.

How was it that we were standing in the parking lot, waiting to find out if my sister was going to rot in jail, and Jax had me not only smiling at him, but chuckling too?

"You're not fooling anyone," I told him.

"What do you mean?"

"You're distracting me so that I won't stress so hard about Charlotte."

He shrugged. "It was working, right?"

"Yes." I stepped into him, holding on tightly and burying my head against his shoulder. "Thank you."

"Any time, Marion. It's what partners do."

Not all partners. I'd seen far too many asshats in my years as a matchmaker. But Jax? He was special. It was too bad we'd wasted so many years apart because I could never believe we were a perfect match. If only I'd taken a leap of faith sooner, I could've had a lifetime of these memories.

"Marion?" Jax gently pulled me away from him. "There she is."

I spun and started to run toward Charlotte, who was walking out with... Denver? He hadn't run? Wow, that was a surprise. But why was he with her, and where was Sebastian?

"Char!" I called.

Her head popped up, and she scanned the parking lot looking for me. Just as our eyes locked, a silver SUV pulled up right next to her. A man in a suit and a trench coat opened a back door for her.

She hesitated, but then gave me a pained look and said, "Take care of Minx for me. I'll call when I can." Then she and Denver got into the car and it took off into the dark night.

"What the hell just happened?" I asked Jax.

"I have no idea. Didn't she just meet that guy? Denver? Is

that his name?" Jax frowned, and everything about him tensed. "What do we know about this guy?"

"Just that Charlotte accidentally cursed him, we healed him, and then their auras matched a deep violet. I've never seen an instant connection like that before. I know they really like each other."

"It's too soon in their relationship to be bailing someone out of jail and then whisking her off so she can't even talk to her family." He started to pace and then ran a hand through his already mussed hair. "We need to find out what happened."

"I couldn't agree more. Let's go." I grabbed his hand and tugged him into the station.

As soon as we were through the door, we ran smack dab into Sebastian.

"Whoa," he said, steadying me. "Are you all right?"

I shook my head. "No. Not at all. I just saw my sister walk out of here with her date, who she's known for only two days. They jumped in a car and sped off. The only thing she told me was to watch her dog. I need to know what the hell is going on."

"You're not the only one," he said, scowling. "I was here waiting for her to sign the papers for me to represent her as her lawyer when they came back and told me she'd accepted different representation and had already been released."

I blinked at him. "What? How? I don't understand. Denver found her a lawyer, and she went with them over you?"

"That's what it sounds like, and since I'm not her lawyer,

they won't tell me anything about the case. I know just about as much as you do." The pulse in his neck ticked.

This was a side of Sebastian I hadn't seen before. Usually he was so calm in a crisis. Very cool. And he never got riled unless it had something to do with Gigi.

"I can't believe this."

"I'll try to find out who her lawyer is through my network and get back to you, but unfortunately, unless she fires them and hires me, then I can't really do anything."

"Except background checks," I said.

"Those I can make happen. Get me everything you can on Denver. I'll have my team start working on it tonight."

"Thank you," I said, sighing in relief. I hadn't realized how worried I was that Denver was a bad actor until Sebastian confirmed my suspicion. "Really. I don't know what we'd do without you."

"I haven't done anything yet," he said. "But I'll do my best."

"I'll leave a voice mail with the details I have on him."

"That works." He gave me a quick hug, shook Jax's hand, and then left.

Jax started to move toward the exit, but I still had business to take care of.

"Hold on." I walked up to the front desk and rang the bell.

A short, round woman with big black plastic rimmed glasses appeared with a coffee mug in her hand. "What can I help you with?"

"I need to see Brix Belford. He's a Magical Task Force agent. He knows me. Tell him Marion Matched is here."

"Ms. Matched, Agent Belford is tied up at the moment. If you want to leave your number, I can give him a message."

"I'm not leaving until I speak to him," I insisted. "I'll just stand right here and wait."

"Your choice," she said, appearing disinterested as she disappeared back into the office.

"Son of a bitch," I growled. "That did not go as planned."

"Marion?" Brix said from behind me.

I spun. "Where did you come from?"

"The coffee room. I heard you demanding to see me."

"And I was told you're too busy. So which is it? Are you available to talk to me, or is that only when you're using my agency as cover for your investigations?"

"I only did that once," he said mildly. "And if you recall, that worked out for both of us."

He had a point, but I was too mad at him to acknowledge it. "Tell me the truth," I demanded. "Did you show up at my agency because you were investigating my sister?"

He didn't answer right away.

"Dammit, Brix! I thought we were friends, and you go and do this? You acted like you were interested in her just to get an invitation to the party. That's low. Really low."

"That's not how it went down," he said quietly.

"Oh, yeah? Then enlighten me." I crossed my arms over my chest. "Tell me how flirting with my sister is all part of the job."

"You *know* that's all part of the job," he said with raised eyebrows.

"Of course I do!" I shouted at him. "Do you think I don't

realize that I'm being unreasonable? Of course an agent would flirt with someone for information. It just galls me that we were friends, that we'd been through some serious shit together, and instead of leveling with me, you used me and my trust to bring down my sister."

He looked stunned for a brief moment before he gripped my arm and said in a loud voice, "I think it's time for you to go, Miss Matched."

I yanked my arm out of his grasp. "I can do that under my own steam. Thanks anyway."

Jax took my hand and, without a word to Brix, led me back outside.

Brix followed, though he kept a bit of distance right up until we'd rounded the corner to where we'd parked. Then he was there with us, his voice lowered. "I'm not supposed to be talking to you about this, understand?"

I nodded.

"Yeah, man," Jax said, placing his hand on the small of my back, a gesture I knew was for support.

"Okay, I'll make this quick. I was in your office looking for Charlotte. Only I had no idea she was your sister. I tracked her here from Portland. None of her identifying information led me to believe she even knew you, much less was related to you. I think someone went to considerable trouble to try to scrub her identity, because all I got was an old address that led back to you and your father many years ago. I was coming to ask you about her, but then there she was. What was I supposed to do? Blow my cover?"

"But, Brix, why were you tracking her in the first place? What did she do?" I asked, afraid to find out the answer.

"That's just it; I don't know for sure yet. All I know is that she's leaving traces of black magic with her signature everywhere she goes. As you are aware, black magic is so dangerous that it's banned in all forms. We need to find out what she's doing with it and why before something catastrophic happens."

"If all that's true, then why didn't you arrest her at my office?"

He chewed on his bottom lip. "The black magic traces weren't showing up on my meter that day. I started to think maybe I had the wrong woman, but tonight when I got to the mixer, they were off the charts. I had no choice. I'm so sorry, Marion."

CHAPTER 16

"I just don't believe that Charlotte would use black magic. She hates that she cursed those people down at Hallucinations," I said to Jax as he pulled his truck into my driveway next to my SUV. I sent a silent thanks to Iris for getting it home for me from Gigi's house.

"Maybe she doesn't know she's using it," he said.

"You mean, maybe someone cursed her with it and she's carrying it around with her?" I asked. But then I shook my head. "It's a decent theory, but something doesn't add up. Brix said his meter didn't register when he was at the office with her. If that's true, then how was it the meter registered tonight?"

"Maybe she was cursed between the time he stopped at the office and when they met again at the mixer," Jax said, still trying to puzzle this out with me.

"But I was with her almost that entire time. I'm not carrying black magic, or I'm sure Brix would've taken me in, too. Plus, Brix said he'd tracked her from Portland. Presumably, she was using it then, too."

"I don't know, Marion. Brix seemed perplexed, too." He leaned over the seats and pressed his palm to my cheek. "We'll figure it out, though."

"We have to." I pulled my phone out, disappointed to see that Charlotte hadn't answered any of my messages. After we left Brix, I'd try to call three times on the way home. All went unanswered. I hit her number and wasn't surprised when it went straight to voice mail. "Why isn't she answering?" I said for the third time.

Jax didn't bother replying. He didn't have the answer, and I didn't expect him to.

"Come on. I need a glass—or bottle—of wine. And all the Pop-Tarts." I pushed my door open, and by the time I was climbing down, Jax was there helping me.

"I'll even toast the Pop-Tarts for you," he said.

I gave him a grateful smile. The man really was too good to be true.

The moment I pushed the door open, Minx came running.

I spotted Ty and Kennedy inside on the couch with Paris Francine curled up next to them.

"Minx has been eyeing that door ever since we came down to raid the cookie jar," Ty said, shaking his head in amusement. "She wasn't even interested in playing with Paris."

"Did you miss me?" I asked Minx. Her little tail was swinging back and forth with excitement right up until she spotted Jax. Then she froze and the growling started.

I was out of patience and placed my hands on my hips. Staring down at her, I said, "Minx, no!"

The growling stopped instantly as she looked at me like, *What the fuck? I was protecting you.*

"I know you think he's a threat of some kind," I said, still talking to Minx. "But I promise you he isn't. You don't have to love him. You don't even have to like him, but you do need to stop growling. And if you try to bite him one more time, we're going to have words, you and I. Understand?"

Minx tilted her head to the side and then, incredibly, she looked at Jax the same exact way.

"Okay, now that we seem to understand each other, you need to let Jax in without ripping another pair of jeans. Understood?"

Minx sat down, looking as sweet as can be.

I laughed and reached down to scoop her up. "You're a character, you know that?"

She answered by licking my cheek.

"Thank you. I love you, too." I strode in, still holding Minx, and went straight to the chair across from Ty and Kennedy, where I curled up with the dog in my lap.

"Wow, that was impressive," Kennedy said, standing and scooping up their Yorkie. "Of course, if you spoke to me like that, I'd probably sit and behave, too."

I rolled my eyes, grateful for the slight reprieve in the otherwise upsetting evening. "Please. I wouldn't speak to you or Ty that way. Well... not unless you needed it."

Kennedy laughed at me then came over and kissed me on the cheek. "We'll get out of your hair."

"Wait," I said. "There's something I have to tell you two."

Kennedy sat back down as Ty moved forward on the couch, giving me his full attention.

"What happened?" Ty asked. He knew me too well. Surely he'd picked up on my distress.

I quickly told them everything that had happened, from Brix arresting Charlotte, to her choosing another lawyer over Sebastian, and then her getting into the car with Denver.

"I can't believe she just took off with a man she's only known for a few days," Ty said, his brows pinched with worry. "That seems... I don't know, like a crazy risk when she had Sebastian trying to help her."

"I agree, but she doesn't know the coven that well. Maybe she thought Denver was her best shot at dealing with this mess." I let out a heavy sigh. "Honestly, I have no idea what she's thinking. She won't pick up and hasn't called me back. I'm hoping that's because she's meeting with a kickass lawyer, but that's just speculation."

Ty sat back with his arms crossed over his chest.

"Black magic," Kennedy whispered and let out a low whistle. "That's intense."

I nodded. "Very. But there's nothing we can do about it tonight. I just thought you should know. Jax and I are going to bed, and we'll try to deal with this in the morning."

Ty stood and held out a hand for Kennedy. "Then we'll get out of your hair. Don't hesitate to let me know if we can help in any way, okay?"

"I will." They each gave me a kiss on the cheek and then quietly slipped out the front door with Paris Francine in tow. I moved to curl up on my couch with Minx in tow.

Jax, who'd been standing against the kitchen doorframe, went into the kitchen, and while Minx kept her gaze fixed on the kitchen door, she didn't even make one peep. It wasn't until he came back into the living room with toasted Pop-Tarts on a plate for me that she let out the tiniest growl.

"Don't think I forgot about you," he said, handing her a mini Greenie. I kept them in the kitchen for Paris Francine when she was visiting. And just like Paris, Minx gobbled it up, even going so far as to lick her chops afterward. "I'm glad you liked it," Jax said before sitting down on the opposite end of the couch.

Minx stiffened, and it was clear she wasn't comfortable with the situation. But she was behaving, so I spent a lot of time scratching her ears and telling her she was a good girl. It took some doing, but eventually she laid between us with her head on a small pillow.

"This dog thinks she owns you," Jax said softly.

"She wouldn't be wrong," I said. "Look at her. The cuteness is overwhelming."

When Minx fell asleep and started snoring softly, I quietly rose from the couch and said, "I'm going to shower. Can you keep an ear out for my phone on the off chance Charlotte calls?"

"Sure. But I'd rather be in that shower with you," he said with a wink.

I grinned, remembering what we'd done the last time we'd showered together. "That would be nice, but..." I glanced at the phone.

"I know. Go on," he said. "We have all night."

"You're staying then?" I asked.

"You couldn't get me to leave if you tried. I wouldn't leave you alone after what happened tonight."

Relief flooded through me. I hadn't even realized that I'd expected him to go home. Usually he didn't, but after the last week of not seeing him much because of his schedule and my sister's unexpected return, I hadn't taken anything for granted. I leaned down and gave him a soft kiss on his cheek. "I'll be quick."

"Take your time," he said and held up a Greenie. "If she wakes up, I'm prepared."

I chuckled softly. "Bribery is an excellent plan."

The shampoo hadn't even been rinsed from my hair when I heard Minx's incessant barking. "Dammit," I muttered and waited a beat as the water sluiced down over me, hoping that Greenie worked. But Minx just continued to bark and carry on as if we had intruders. I ducked under the spray, rushing to get the shampoo out of my long red hair. Once I was done, I reached for the tap to turn the water off, but the barking had stopped.

When I didn't hear Minx again, I sent a silent *thank you* to the universe and lingered in the shower until my fingers started to prune.

Warm and happy in my flannel pajama bottoms and a T-shirt, I went to rescue Jax. Only when I found him on the couch, Minx was curled up on his chest, her head snuggled underneath his chin, both of them sound asleep.

My heart melted right then and there. I had no idea what he'd done to calm Minx down, but he was clearly a genius.

After finding my phone and taking multiple photos, I whispered, "Hey, sleepyhead."

Jax's eyes fluttered open. His voice was groggy as he said, "Hey yourself."

I stared pointedly at the dog, still sound asleep.

He chuckled. "It turns out that Hagrid was right."

"What? Who's that?"

"Never mind. All I needed to do was figure out what calmed her." He pointed to the pink sweatshirt that Minx was curled up on. "It's Charlotte's. The moment I got close to her with this, she started sniffing it and then whined as if she was missing her mom. At first, I put it on my chest to protect myself from getting attacked because it kept distracting her. But eventually she just laid down and closed her eyes. Now we're… I dunno if besties is the right word, but I think we have an understanding."

I shook my head in amazement. "You're brilliant."

"If you say so. But maybe not, because it looks like this dog is sleeping with us."

I just nodded. He was right. There was no way I was putting her in Charlotte's room by herself all night. If she'd been crate trained that would be one thing, but she wasn't. She slept with Charlotte. With her gone, the dog was always going to have a place with me. "She's tiny. How much space can she take up?"

Jax laughed. "You're going to eat those words."

As it turned out, tiny Chihuahuas can take up almost an entire side of a king-size bed. And no, she didn't sleep on one side. She slept right between us. I woke in the morning to find Jax two miles away on the other side of the room.

Meanwhile, Minx was stretched out longways and was licking my face while thumping her tail on Jax's.

He moaned and rolled over.

"Chicken," I said and snuggled into Minx, enjoying her affection.

Then I thought about Charlotte, grabbed my phone, saw that she hadn't called, and groaned. "How long did Sebastian say it would take for the background check?" I asked Jax.

"He said it depends on how much information you have on Denver. Most take a few days, but some of his tougher cases have taken as long as a full week."

"Please don't let it take that long," I said, throwing an arm over my eyes.

His tone was pained when he added, "Especially if we have a Chihuahua sleeping between us every night."

I reached over and patted his cheek, but Minx pounced on me, love bombing me with kisses all over my face. I was laughing when I said, "There's always the shower."

CHAPTER 17

*J*t had been five days since Charlotte had been
arrested. Sebastian still didn't have the results of
Denver's background check, and I was running out of ideas
on how to find my sister. At day three, the coven had
convened to try a finding spell. If she wouldn't or couldn't
call, maybe we could at least get an idea of where she was.
But nothing. There'd been no hint of where she might be.
We'd all decided maybe it was the black magic that was
blocking our efforts.

The sun was just about to rise as I stood on the beach
staring out at the vast ocean, yearning for answers.

"We're going to find her," Dad said. "We will."

I squeezed his hand, comforted by his presence. I'd been
having trouble sleeping. Every morning, I'd woken before
dawn, pacing my house with Minx still cuddled up in bed
with Jax. The little dog had really taken to him since the
night Charlotte disappeared. The two of them were

practically inseparable. They were adorable, and I was grateful. If I'd had to deal with a snarling dog while going out of my mind with worry, I'd have had a nervous breakdown by now.

"Thanks for coming this morning," I told Dad. I couldn't take one more minute of being in my cottage and had decided to head to the beach. Knowing Dad was an early riser, I'd texted him on the way and asked if he'd join me. I'd been strong all week, but I just needed to be with someone who loved Charlotte as much as I did.

"Anything for my Marionberry." He usually used the nickname lightly, but this morning there was pain in his tone. He was also hurting.

"Have you talked to Liana? Does she know what's going on?"

He let out a sigh. "Yes. Have you?"

I shook my head. "I don't have anything to say to her."

"Marion, I know your mother hurt you, but holding on to all that resentment forever isn't healthy."

There were a few things I wanted to ask him, and although I wasn't sure this was the right time, I just needed to know. "After she left, when did you start talking to her again?"

Dad stood with his hands in his pockets, rocking back on his feet. When he finally looked over at me, he said, "About two months."

I gaped. "*Two months?* And you never told me? Just... why? After what she did, how could you possibly have let her back in?"

"I had Charlotte. Do you really think I should have not

spoken to her? Your mom wanted to know how she was doing. She deserved to at least know that Charlotte was safe, even if she was hurt and missing her mom."

I noticed that my dad didn't say anything about my mother asking about me. It was a selfish, ridiculous thought. I'd been a grown woman with my own business by then. Of course my mother didn't need to keep tabs on me. But Charlotte had just been eight years old. "I guess I'm glad she at least cared how Charlotte was doing after she abandoned her."

Dad's fingers tightened around mine. "She always called me to ask about you when she left the first time. Did you know that?"

I shook my head, my heart aching. How could a woman just leave her children like that? I'd been older than Charlotte when my mother left Dad the first time. But I still didn't understand it. I was a teenager, just on the cusp of figuring out my life. Looking back now, it was a time when I'd thought I didn't need her. I was self-righteous and ready to start living. How naive I was. I let out a sardonic chuckle. "Teenagers always think they've got it all figured out, don't they?"

"They do," he agreed with a warm smile.

"Meanwhile most of us are just bumbling idiots who don't know shit about life yet and could use a lot of guidance. She wasn't there for me then, you know."

"That's true. I think she had her own demons to battle."

I turned, my eyes flashing with anger. "That's no excuse for leaving! You didn't. You'd never in a million years have left your family. I just don't... ah, fuck!"

"Don't what, Marion?" Dad asked softly.

"I needed her and she wasn't there. She was selfish and still is."

"That's true," he agreed mildly.

"But yet, even after all this time, you talk to her still. Charlotte and I are grown women. She doesn't need to be calling you to find out about us. If she wants to be in our lives, then she has to do the work to get to know us, to put us first for once." There was no more heat in my tone when I asked, "Why do you put up with it?"

Dad sucked in a deep breath and let it out slowly. "You're right. She should work on her relationship with the two of you. Liana doesn't need to be calling me for information on how your life is going. Though she does, and I feel obligated to let her know that her daughter is thriving." A proud smile claimed his lips. "You're an absolute joy to know, Marion."

I reached over and gave him a sideways hug. "It's all because of you."

"I wish I could take credit, but it's all yours, Marionberry."

We stood there for a few beats, watching the surf crash against the beach before Dad pulled away and stared me in the eye. "I don't want you to think that the only reason I talk to your mom is because of you and Charlotte."

I raised my eyebrows, wondering where the heck this was going. If he was about to tell me some bullshit about never getting over her, I was going to scream. My mother was a walking relationship disaster and Dad deserved so much better.

"I talk to her because I loved her once. Just because our

relationship didn't survive, that doesn't mean that love just goes away."

"Oh, goddess. You're still holding out hope that she'll come back to you, aren't you? Is that why you've been so reluctant to commit to someone else all these years? I always thought it was because you were afraid of getting hurt again, that you were protecting yourself."

"What?" His face morphed into pure confusion. "You think I'm pining for your mother?" He laughed. Actually laughed. "Oh, Marion. No. The day she left without even telling me while leaving Charlotte in my care, that was the final straw. I wanted to make it work when she came home with Charlotte in tow. Having our family back together was worth the effort of trying to repair the wreckage of our relationship. But there was no coming back from that twice."

"But you said you still love her. After everything she's done, how can that be true?" I was genuinely curious. I was fairly certain that if the man I'd loved had left me not once, but twice, any love I'd felt for him would have quickly burned away.

He shrugged one shoulder. "I'm not in love with her. But the person that I fell in love with all those years ago is still in there. You don't just stop loving people because they disappoint you. Not usually, anyway. And remember, my relationship with her is different than the one you have with her. I wasn't a saint when we were together. Both of us contributed to the demise of our marriage." He placed one hand on my cheek, his steady gaze holding mine. "I can't apologize enough for what that's done to you."

"You don't have to apologize to me, Dad. I was never angry that you two split up. Did I like it? Of course not. No one wants to see their parents get divorced. I was angry and hurt because Mom left me and chose someone else over our family. Over me. And she did it again and again throughout the years. She's not my safe place. You are. You're the one whose been here the whole time. No matter what, I always know you'll be here when I need you. You're the person I go to when I need a safe place to land. You have no idea what a gift that is."

"Come here." Dad pulled me into his chest and hugged me for a long time. "I know you're worrying yourself to death about Charlotte, but try not to panic until there's something concrete to worry about. Your mother says she'll be all right. Charlotte is like a cat; she always lands on her feet."

"Cats only have nine lives, Dad," I said, not bothering to hid my sarcasm. "What does Liana know about it anyway?"

"I don't know, but she seems to think that Denver can help Charlotte."

"Of course she does," I said automatically. "Mom always did think that a man could fix all her problems."

He sighed. "Okay, enough about Liana." He pulled away. "Tazia wanted me to give you a message."

I perked up at that. Tazia just knew things sometimes. "What is it?"

"She said in order to find Charlotte, you need to remember your connection and that you're stronger together."

I swallowed my sigh of disappointment. I should've

known. Tazia's messages were almost never straightforward. "We already tried a finding spell. The coven didn't have any success."

"I know. I was just relaying what she said." He jerked his head toward the empty beach in front of us. "Come on. Let's finish this walk so you can get home to that breakfast Jax is making for you."

I frowned at him. "What makes you think Jax is making me breakfast?"

Dad winked at me. "Just a hunch."

"You two are up to something, aren't you?"

My dad just chuckled. "You never were good with surprises.

CHAPTER 18

"Something is bothering me and I don't know what it is," I said to Jax as I stabbed a piece of homemade waffle.

"Is it that Minx loves me more than you?" he teased and scratched the dog's ears.

Incredibly, when I'd gotten home, I'd had two surprises. One was the waffle and bacon breakfast with homemade biscuits. The other was Jax wearing a puppy sling with Minx tucked into it against his chest. Her little head was poking out, her eyes curious as she watched the world from her new vantage point.

"I still don't understand why Minx is wrapped up in that carrier," I said, eyeing them both. "Did you just miss snuggling me this morning, so you forced her into that thing while you were working in the kitchen?"

Jax snorted. "Minx is no substitute for you, Marion. Trust me. And I told you, she kept whining that she wanted to be held, but I couldn't cook breakfast while doing her bidding, so I put her in this."

"Yes, but where did you get that carrier?" I asked, narrowing my eyes at him. "I highly doubt it's Charlotte's. If she had one, it would be pink and full of sparkles. That one is basic black and actually camouflages Minx a little too much. Charlotte would want to show off how adorable they both were if she wore one of those things."

His face flushed as he mumbled, "I might have picked it up yesterday."

"Why?" I asked, laughing.

"I thought she might want to go on a walk with us in the evening, but she won't last that long with her tiny legs, so I got this. Looks like she likes it."

I shook my head. "You're a goner."

"You're right about that." He kissed the top of Minx's head, and she returned the favor by licking his chin.

"I've lost you both to each other."

"Nah," he reassured me. "We both still love you. We still allow you to get into bed at night," he teased.

"Thanks. I feel so… treasured."

Jax reached over and squeezed my thigh. "You are. Now, back to what you were saying before you decided to bust my balls about Minx. Something doesn't feel right. Any hints?"

"Right." I took another bite of my waffle before I continued. "This is fantastic by the way."

"Thanks. The more praise I get, the more breakfasts you'll get in the future."

"I like the way you think," I said but quickly sobered as I

answered his question. "Something about the conversation I had with my dad about Charlotte this morning isn't sitting right."

Jax put his fork down and leaned forward. "What did he say about Charlotte?"

"Well, Tazia told him to tell me to remember our connection and that we're stronger together." I took a sip of coffee and placed the mug back on the table. "But that doesn't help me. If we're not together, my magic is useless to help her. And the coven already tried a finding spell. I don't know what else to do. It's not like we can communicate telepathically."

Jax raised his eyebrows. "There might be ways to do that, though, right?"

"None that I know of," I said. "I'm new to the full-fledged witch thing, remember? My aura-reading ability was all I knew until very recently. I'm mostly relying on the coven to give me ideas on how we might find her."

"What about calling Hollister?" Jax asked, sounding a little incredulous, as if I should've thought to call him first. "He owns a magic store and knows practically everything about spelling objects and creating potions. I bet he at least has some ideas to try."

"Jax, I think you might be a genius," I said as I stared at him, wondering why I hadn't thought of that. Hollister was the brother of a former client of mine, and he was the one who'd helped me find both Kennedy and his future sister-in-law when they'd gone missing. We hadn't gotten along at first, but by the end of the ordeal, we'd become good friends.

"I do my best." He smirked at me and then fed Minx the tiniest piece of bacon.

"She's gonna be a huge beggar if you keep that up," I said.

"She already is. Charlotte made sure of that. For all her talk about Minx's special diet, I saw her sneak this dog treats from practically every meal Charlotte ate."

At the mention of Charlotte's name, suddenly my thoughts shifted into focus. "I've got it! Now I know why my conversation with Dad is bothering me so much."

"Well, are you gonna tell me or should I start guessing?" Jax asked.

"He said that my mom told him she thinks Denver can help Charlotte. How would she know that? But more importantly, how does she know about Denver at all? Charlotte just met him, and Charlotte and my mom are no contact. It doesn't make any sense."

"Did your dad tell her about Denver?" Jax asked.

"Maybe, but all Dad knew was that he and Charlotte were just getting to know each other and that Denver was there when she was released from jail. Why would my mother think anything about Denver based on those details? I just feel like maybe she knows something that I don't."

"Why don't you just ask her?" Jax reasoned.

"That would mean calling her," I said petulantly.

He chuckled softly. "Are you gonna dial, or am I?"

"I hate you sometimes, you know that, right?"

"No you don't," Jax said, brushing a lock of my hair off my brow.

"Fine, I don't. But I am still irritated you suggested this because now I have to call or it's going to drive me insane."

Jax handed me my phone. "Minx and I are going to go clean up the kitchen."

"Now you're just talking dirty to me. You do know that there is nothing sexier than a man who cooks and cleans, right?"

"Whatever gets you worked up." He blew me a kiss as he carried our empty plates back into the kitchen.

I stared at my phone, semi-wishing it would die so I'd have an excuse to put this off. But finding Charlotte was too important to let my anger at my mother get in the way. I closed my eyes, said a silent prayer that this call didn't go sideways, and then hit Liana's number.

The phone rang four times before my mother picked it up. "Oh my goddess, you're alive," she said by way of greeting.

"Is there a reason I wouldn't be?" I asked.

"Well, who knows?" my mother said with a sniff. "I figured I'd hear from you before now. Apologies go over better if they aren't dragged out, you know."

"You wanted me to call so you could apologize?" I asked, feeling a little shocked and somewhat confused. My mother never apologized unless it was in the heat of the moment when she said, *Fine! I apologize! Happy now?*

"What? No. Why would I have to apologize?" she asked. "You and Charlotte are the ones who practically threw me out when all I wanted was talk to you. I think I'm the one who is owed an apology."

175

"We tried to talk to you!" I insisted. "At the Bird's Eye Café. You stood us up."

She hesitated. "I had something come up. I tried to reschedule, but you refused to call me back. So, Marion, what is it you want from me?"

"I want to know how you know about Denver," I said.

"What do you mean?" she asked. "Oh, you mean that guy your sister is dating?"

"They aren't dating, but they were on a date the night she was arrested. What do you know about him, and why did you tell Dad you think he can help her?"

"Because he can," she said. "Now, it's time for me to ask you a question."

"About?" I asked, my stomach starting to tighten into knots. I'd really only wanted to get a few answers from her and then end the call. This was starting to sound like she was going to manipulate the conversation, just like she did with everything else.

"I just want to know why we can't move past everything," she said, her voice quavering with emotion.

"Just move past everything?" I echoed. "How exactly are we supposed to do that?"

"You could stop punishing me for something I did when I was young and stupid." She sniffed and let out a tiny sob. "I don't really deserve to lose both of my daughters just because your dad and I got divorced, do I?"

"You aren't losing me because you got a divorce," I said, not quite believing I was having this conversation for the second time today. Though at least with Dad, we hadn't been confrontational. I suspected that this exchange with my mother was going to be anything but respectful on either of our parts.

"It sure seems that way." Her voice was small and barely a whisper.

"I'm angry because you left me. And then you left me and Charlotte to be with a man who never treated you right. You chose him over us time and time and time again. Remember when you couldn't help me with my grand opening when I first started Miss Matched?"

"I had to cancel because Arlo needed me to drive him—"

"To his poker game," I said, cutting her off. "I know. You've told me that before. But my grand opening was very important to me. You chose taking him to a poker game over spending time with me. It hurt."

"I already said I was sorry for that," my mother whined. "How many times do I have to say it?"

It would never be enough because her words meant nothing. Not when she kept repeating the same patterns. "You don't have to say it again, Mother. I just need you to show me that I'm important in your life instead of always being second place to a man. Not just Arlo, but any man. Do you have any idea how many times you canceled plans with me to go out with Arlo?"

"I—" Liana started.

I cut off whatever she was going to say. "Don't, Mother. Just think about what I said."

"Fine.'" Her tone was curt and obviously defensive. "I'll think about it. But you think about this; if you want information from me about Charlotte, then you can get it from me *after* you agree to have dinner with me this Saturday night at Witches' Garden."

"Are you blackmailing me to have dinner with you instead of answering questions about my sister, who hasn't been seen in *five days?*" I asked, shocked at her callousness, yet also not surprised at all. My mother had always been known for doing whatever was necessary to get her way. Even when we were talking about Charlotte being MIA.

"No, I'm not blackmailing you, Marion. Why do you have to be so dramatic?"

"Then tell me how you know about Denver," I blurted.

"Are we on for dinner?" she asked, sounding smug, like she just knew she'd get her way.

"Fine," I growled. "But you're telling me what you know about Denver before we end this call, understood?"

I could practically hear her roll her eyes. "I know because I spoke to her. She's fine, Marion. I'm sure as soon as she's figured out this nonsense charge, she'll be back for good. Until then, you should stop worrying about her. You know how she is. Charlotte just goes off the grid when she's upset. Like that day she turned eighteen and just took off. She's impulsive and hotheaded. That can be both good and bad."

"She was arrested and there are likely charges of using black magic pending, and you're over here telling me she's just impulsive?" I asked, ready for this conversation to be over. My mother was being less than helpful. Besides, even if Charlotte had just taken off, she wouldn't have left Minx. I was positive about that.

"Arrested doesn't mean charged, Marion," my mother

said. "Stop being such a downer. You must've gotten that from your dad."

"In that case, I'm honored to be the resident downer," I said sarcastically.

"Suit yourself. See you Saturday. Your treat since you're so successful now," she said.

I knew she was trying to be funny, but the joke went over like a lead balloon. This was a dinner I didn't want to go to, and the only reason I didn't tell her to shove her dinner where the sun didn't shine was that I wanted to be in contact with her if she heard from Charlotte again.

"Mom?" I said, using the word I hadn't used in over two decades while addressing her.

"Yes, baby," she said, sounding teary again.

"Will you let me know if you hear from Charlotte again?"

Liana's voice was flat when she answered. "Yeah, sure."

"I just want to know she's safe," I added, because somehow, she'd managed to make me feel guilty for caring more about what was going on with my sister than I did about the conversation my mother and I had just had.

That ache in my stomach was starting to grow the longer I spoke with her. I made a mental note to ask my doctor to check it out on my next visit.

"Charlotte is fine," Liana said in a stern voice. "I promise you Denver will make sure of that."

"Do you know Denver?" I asked her, suddenly suspicious. "Have you met him?"

"No!" she said just a little too quickly.

"Why don't I believe you?" I asked.

She sighed. "Fine, Marion. You win. I have met him. But you'll have to wait until dinner for me to tell you all about it. See you then, and Marion?"

"Yes?"

"Don't be late. You always were the pokey one."

The line went dead before I had a chance to tell her to go to hell. This was why I never spoke to her anymore. Everything was all about her. Always. Every time.

Even when my sister was MIA.

CHAPTER 19

J was just about to call Hollister when my front door burst open and Kennedy came striding in. "Marion, Ty found Eli."

My head jerked up as the phone slipped from my grip and onto the floor in front of my chair. "You mean the guy Charlotte followed to Premonition Pointe? That Eli?"

"Yes." He passed his phone to me. There was a text from Ty confirming the news.

"How?" Charlotte and I had tried to find him as soon as we realized our power could reverse the curse. But he hadn't answered her calls, and he hadn't been at home any of the three times we'd gone by his apartment. I scrolled the few messages Ty had exchanged with Kennedy. There wasn't much, other than he'd met Eli and the man was demanding that Charlotte and I reverse his curse. *If only*, I thought with a sigh. Then I scrolled one more time and found a sext from earlier in the week that was definitely not safe for mother figures. "Whoa. Sorry. Didn't mean to intrude."

"Oh, fuck me," Kennedy said under his breath as his cheeks flushed. "I forgot that was there."

I nodded, trying to wipe the sexts from my mind. "No worries. It's good to know you two have a healthy sex life."

"Oh, hell. Please don't ever say anything like that again," he pleaded.

"No promises," I said with a laugh. "You guys should know better than most that I can't control the advice when it seems relevant."

"I'm dying right now," he said dramatically.

"If people died from embarrassment, I'm sorry to say that Ty would've dropped dead a long time ago."

Kennedy pressed his hand to his forehead. "Thank the gods he survived."

The phone pinged.

Kennedy read it and glanced up. "Ty and Eli are on their way here."

"They are?" Panic crawled at my throat. I wasn't going to be able to help the man, and I hated that I was going to have to disappoint him. However, he could be a valuable source of information. Since Charlotte had dated him recently, it was possible he might have some idea how she'd managed to get involved with black magic.

The front door banged open and a man with a red-spotted face strode in. "Where is she?"

"She who? Charlotte?" I asked as Ty walked in behind him.

"Yeah, Charlotte. She's the one who did this to me, right?

The breakout happened the night I told her I wasn't interested in dating anymore. She touched me, and I had some sort of weird regret, followed by an intense stomachache. At first I thought the breakout was caused by stress, but then it kept getting worse and worse."

"You must be Eli," I said, holding my hand out to him.

He ignored it and narrowed his eyes when he spotted Minx, who was at my feet on full alert with her ears back.

"I already told him she wasn't here," Ty said.

"Then I'll wait." Eli sat down on the couch and patted the space next to him. Minx promptly ran and jumped up beside him. When he started petting her, she leaned into him and looked up at him with adoring eyes.

I raised my eyebrows. "You two know each other pretty well."

"Me and Charlotte?" he asked, sounding confused. "We dated for about a month. I guess knowing her well is relative."

"No. I meant you and Minx." I nodded to the dog.

"Oh." He smiled softly as he looked down at her. "We're good friends. In fact, I met Minx before I met Charlotte at a dog park."

I was starting to get the impression that Charlotte met a lot of men at the dog parks. Which, thinking it through, wasn't a bad plan. Dog lovers tended to have big hearts, and that was a giant plus in the dating column.

"When will she be back?" Eli asked, his gaze darting around the room.

"We don't know," I said.

Eli scowled. "Listen, I've just gotten back in town after

going to LA to try some remedies for this tragedy, and learned from an acquaintance that you two have been fixing this for other people." He pointed to his face. "If she doesn't reverse this immediately, I'm going to report her to the Magical Task Force and then file a civil suit for damages. Did you know I'm a model?"

I winced. That meant he'd been out of work for well over a week.

"How am I supposed to book jobs looking like this? I've already had to turn down three. I've tried everything. Creams, elixirs, fasting, facials. Nothing works. It's not getting better. And after finding out I'm not the only one with this problem, it's going to be one hell of a class action lawsuit. Charlotte will be paying for this for the rest of her life."

"Charlotte wants to help you," I said. "Didn't you get her messages?"

"I deleted them," he said, crossing his arms over his chest. "I didn't want to hear from her."

Understandable. I'd have been icing someone out if they cursed me, too. I cleared my throat. "The problem is she's MIA at the moment, and we don't know where she is or if she can get in contact with us."

He narrowed his eyes. "What the hell does that mean? I know she helped some other people. I saw their before and after photos."

I really didn't want to give him any information about her arrest and how she'd disappeared right after. That would only give him more ammunition for his lawsuit if he went through with it. But I needed information, and maybe if I was honest with him, he'd reciprocate. "It appears that Charlotte might have been unknowingly caught up with some bad actors."

He stared me in the eye. "I'm listening."

"I don't know a lot, but I definitely know she didn't mean to curse you. In fact, she was trying to hit you with a love spell."

His eyes widened in shock. "What? When I was trying to break up with her?"

Grimacing, I nodded. "Apparently she really liked you. Cursing you was definitely not the plan. She felt terrible about it. That's why we tried so hard to find you, but since you were out of town and not answering her calls, we were at a loss."

"A love spell. Fucking hell." He shook his head in disbelief. "I always knew she was selfish, but this... That's not right."

"I agree and told her as much," I said, trying to gain his trust. Or at least make it so he didn't storm out.

"So what's the solution? I'm just like this until you find her? Unless *you* can fix me. I did hear that you two were the ones making the rounds to reverse this thing."

"I wish I could. Believe me. But the magic only seems to work when we're together," I said.

"Try anyway," he demanded. "I can't keep living like this." He waved both hands in front of his face. "If this isn't cleared up, I'm not going to make rent, and then I'll be a homeless bastard whose life is ruined just because some crazy bitch couldn't take rejection."

Ouch. Again, he wasn't wrong.

"If I promise to try, will you answer some questions for me?" I asked. "I'm trying to figure out what's going on with Charlotte and why this happened, so hopefully it never happens again."

"I don't think you're in a position to be bargaining, do you?"

"No. If I were in your shoes, I'd be just as angry. But I was hoping to appeal to your empathetic side. If I can find her, we can reverse this for everyone and hopefully find a way to make sure this never happens again."

"You mean by making sure she doesn't cast love spells on anyone again?" He slammed his eyes shut and muttered, "Hasn't she ever heard of consent?"

Brutal. But it wasn't anything I hadn't already told Charlotte myself. "I don't think she'll be casting any spells *ever* again to be honest. I'm not excusing her. Not in the least. I'm just trying to right a wrong and make sure she's safe. If my suspicions are correct, then Charlotte was cursed herself and that's why this all happened in the first place."

"It happened because she cast an unwanted love spell on someone who was no longer interested," he spat out.

"Yes, it did. But the curse only happened because someone else cursed her. And it appears to be a much more evil crime than Charlotte's love spell." I knew that love spells only really worked on people who wanted them to. They were sort of like a suggestion, and if the person was interested it gave them motivation to take things further. If they weren't, then the spell would fall flat. It sounded as if that's exactly what would have happened if the love spell had worked correctly. Eli would've had a moment where he was questioning what he was doing in breaking things off with her, but then he would've moved on. While I maintained that love spells were unethical and would never subject anyone to them, they weren't going to force someone to do something they didn't want to do. But explaining all that to Eli seemed like a wasted effort. He was too mad, and rightly so.

"Someone cursed her?" he asked. His brows furrowed as he glanced down, appearing to be in thought.

"Yes. I'm certain of it. While my sister can be impulsive and a little selfish, she isn't the type of person who wants to hurt anyone," I said quietly.

He nodded, and I started to feel like we were getting somewhere. "That's true. All of it. That's why I've been so pissed about this curse. It's just so vindictive and not at all like the person I thought she was."

"It's not. I promise she's been very upset by this and wants to make it right again."

His head jerked up, and there was fire in his eyes when he said, "I told her that talisman was bad news. If she'd have just dumped it, this probably never would've happened."

"Talisman?" I asked. "What talisman?"

"That pendant she wore. It was an evil-looking eye. I always felt like it was staring at me. I told her it was creepy, but she said she wore it for protection. That it made her feel safer. Safer from what, I wasn't sure."

"Evil-looking eye?" Kennedy asked. "Are you sure it was a pendant and not a bracelet charm?" He and Ty had been sitting back listening to the entire conversation. I'd almost forgotten they were there.

"It was definitely a pendant," Eli said. "I told her not to wear it around me because it made me uncomfortable. She agreed. I never saw it again after that."

"She wears an eye on a charm bracelet. It's the only charm on it," Kennedy said.

"She does?" I asked, not remembering any charm bracelet. And I'd be in the position to know since we'd spent most days together, trying to find the men she'd accidentally cursed.

"Yeah. She was wearing it the night of the mixer." Kennedy pulled out his phone and swiped to a picture of her and Minx in the living room. It looked like Kennedy had taken her picture just before she left for Gigi's. "Look."

I enlarged the photo and could just barely make out the charm. It was definitely an eye.

Eli squinted at it. "That's a match to the pendant," he said with a nod. "I wonder if she was wearing it the night we met at Hallucinations?"

Was the evil-eye talisman cursed with black magic? Would that explain why Brix didn't feel the magic the day we'd been in the office but did at the mixer? It was a decent theory. "Eli, do you have any idea where she got that pendant and charm bracelet?"

He shook his head. "No. She just showed up with it one day, and when I asked where she got it, she said that it was a gift from a family friend she hadn't seen in years. They'd had dinner together the night before, but that was all she told me and then quickly changed the subject."

Family friend? Who in the hell could that be? I had no idea. Dad hadn't had a lot of friends, just a lot of women he'd dated after my mother left. But none of them had lasted long enough to become anything other than a distant memory. Was it an old school friend? Maybe. At least that was a lead I hadn't had before.

"I really don't know anything else," Eli said. "I think it's time for you to hold up your end of the bargain."

"Right," I said, dreading how this was going to go. I hadn't tried to heal anyone since Charlotte had gone missing, since every time we'd done it before, my magic hadn't even sparked until Charlotte and I were touching. "Okay, I'm willing to give this a go, but know that I won't be surprised if it doesn't work."

"Fine. Just try it."

I walked over to him, brought my hand up, and touched his face.

Nothing. Not even a spark of magic.

I dropped my hand and thought about magic filling my fingertips. A tiny spark tingled in my palm, and I pressed my hand to his face again, concentrating on what it felt like when Charlotte and I did this together.

The magic vanished.

"It's not working," I said, sounding defeated.

"You've barely even tried," he said. "I'm not leaving until you give this a real effort. Do it again," he ordered.

His tone made me straighten my spine with indignation. He made it sound as if I'd barely given this any effort, and maybe that's exactly what it looked like. But I knew deep in my bones what it felt like to heal someone, and that spark of magic that I shared with Charlotte just didn't exist on my own.

"Hold on. Let me try something," I said and hurried into Charlotte's room. I glanced around, looking for something that would help me connect with her. There wasn't much. Just a toiletries bag on the dresser and some clothes hanging in the closet. I quickly rummaged through the toiletry bag and let out a whoop when I found a ring my dad had given her for her sixteenth birthday. The stone was a small red ruby heart, the kind that had been available for reasonable prices at most mall jewelry stores. I hadn't seen Charlotte wear it once since she'd walked back into my life ten days ago, but the fact that she traveled with it meant it still had meaning for her.

I slipped the ring onto my pinky finger and walked back out into the living room. After grabbing my dagger, I stood in front of Eli again. This time when I thought of Charlotte and our connection, magic sprang to life between my palm and the hilt of my dagger. The dagger turned blue like it always did when I needed it.

"There," Eli said, pointing at the light. "It's working."

Maybe it was and maybe it wasn't, but we wouldn't know for sure until I tried.

Clutching my dagger and palming Eli's cheek, the magic that had come to life sprang from my fingertips and washed over Eli's face. That tingle I usually felt with Charlotte was there, but it was much fainter, and I struggled to keep the magic flowing. It flickered, the light weakening and strengthening and then flashing out for good.

I glanced at the dagger, finding the blue light gone. And no matter how much I willed it to return, there was no response.

With my shoulders slumped, I took a step back and glanced up at Eli, an apology already forming on my lips. But when I focused, I noted that the redness was gone, though the bumps still hadn't fully retreated.

"Did it work?" he asked, pressing his fingertips to his face and frowning. "How could it not work? I felt the magic. It made my skin tingle, and I was just sure it was doing something."

"It did work... sort of," Ty said. "It's better than it was."

I nodded. "It is, but I'm sorry I couldn't cure you completely." I held my hand up. "It appears I've used everything I've got trying."

Eli ran for the hall bathroom, and when he returned there was a look of determination on his face. "I'll be back tomorrow. We'll try again then."

"I don't—" I started.

"You'll try again, or I'm calling my lawyer," he said.

I shrugged. "Okay. I'll try." There was no harm in that, right?

"I'll be here at eight." Eli spun on his heel and strode out the door, his head held high.

"That was..." Ty started.

"Impressive?" Kennedy offered.

"More like crazy," I said. "I have no idea what is happening, but we need to figure out where that eye charm came from. If we can do that, we might be able to get some answers about how and why Charlotte seems to be cursed with black magic."

CHAPTER 20

*J*ax's name flashed on my phone just as I pulled into the parking lot of Crooner's Cauldron. I quickly hit Accept. "Hey. You got my message."

"Just now. What's this about you driving to LA?"

"I talked to Hollister about spells to find Charlotte, and he said if I could get down here with a few of her personal items, he'd do his best to help me."

"You're already there?" he asked, sounding incredulous.

"Well, yeah. I was leaving when I left you that message." Now that I had the information from Eli that Charlotte's black magic problem was probably coming from a talisman, I wanted to figure out where it had come from before I told Brix about it. I wanted proof she was an innocent who'd been set up so that there was no chance she took the fall for someone else. "Hollister freelances for the Magical Task Force and knows a hell of a lot about illegal spells and potions. After you suggested I call him, I figured he was my best bet."

"I just wish you'd waited for me is all," he said. "I don't like you getting caught up in black magic stuff. We don't know who did this or why."

"That's why I'm here asking the best for help," I said, getting a little impatient. "Don't worry. I'll be back tonight."

"You know I'm going to worry anytime you're doing magic. Especially if you're going to take on a black magic user. What am I supposed to do? Just go back to work and not worry about you?"

My irritation vanished. It wasn't fun being the one waiting to see what happened to your loved one when they ran head first into a problem without thinking through what it could mean for their safety. And unfortunately, I seemed to do that a lot these days. "I'm not planning to deal with any black magic users. I promise. I just want answers I can hand over to Brix and let him deal with the bad guys."

There was silence on the other end of the line.

"Jax, seriously. I just want to find my sister and get her home. That's all." I didn't for one minute believe that she wanted to be wherever she was. Even if she was okay with ditching me and Dad again, she wouldn't leave Minx. She loved that dog far too much.

"Okay, but please call me when you're on your way home. I'm going to be distracted until I have you back in my arms."

My heart melted. "I will. And I promise, I won't go looking for trouble."

"You know, Marion, I believe that you believe that. Trouble just seems to find you."

I had no argument because that was true. Instead, I said, "I'll be careful. I promise."

"Glad to hear it. I'll meet you at your place later?"

"Minx will be waiting for you," I said softly.

"We'll *both* be waiting for you. Drive safely. Don't forget to call when you're back on the road."

"I won't." We said our goodbyes and then I jumped out of the car, grabbed the bag of Charlotte's personal items, and hurried into Hollister's shop.

The scent of lavender and vanilla washed over me the moment I walked through the front door. Herbs and recipe books lined the wall to the right while aisles and aisles of candles, crystals, and other various tools such as mortars and pestles, small daggers, and potion bottles filled the rest of the store. I was fairly certain that if a witch were looking for something to complete a spell or potion, this was the place to find it.

"Well, well, well, look who finally decided it was time to grace us with her presence."

I turned and spotted Hollister leaning against the doorframe that led to another room in the shop. He wore jeans, a fitted white button-down shirt, and soft leather shoes. His dark curly hair was styled with just enough product to tame it, but not enough to make him look too polished. While he didn't look corporate, he didn't exactly look the part of a powerful witch either. It was an outfit I'd expect a salesman to wear.

"You'd probably sell more merchandise if you dressed

like a badass warlock. You know that, right?" I said with a teasing smile.

He chuckled. "Business is just fine, but if sales start to drop off, I'll break out my cloak."

"You have a cloak?" I asked, incredulous. "And you're not wearing it for me? I'm so disappointed."

"It's being pressed for the séance later tonight."

"Seriously?" I asked, not sure if he was pulling my leg. But then his eyes glinted with amusement, making me roll mine. "You're terrible."

"You're just too easy to rile up." He winked at me and then opened his arms, waiting for a hug.

I walked into his embrace and grinned up at him. "It's good to see you."

"You too, Marion." He let me go, glanced at my bag, and said, "This way."

I followed him into the adjoining room and let out a cry of happiness when I spotted Kiera and Garrison sitting on a desk, holding hands. I'd met Kiera when she was on the run from her evil ex, who just happened to be Brix's brother, and eventually had set the pair up. They'd just gotten married and looked every bit the part of newlyweds who were still in that honeymoon phase.

"Marion!" Kiera ran over to me, and the two of us stood there hugging for a long moment. When we pulled apart, both of us had tears in our eyes.

"It's so good to see you," I said and then nodded at Garrison.

"You look amazing." Kiera gave me a knowing smile. "You have a glow about you that you didn't have when you lived here in LA. Can I assume that has something to do with that hot contractor you've been dating?"

I laughed. "That, or I'm just spending too much time in the sun."

We quickly caught up on each other's lives, and then when the bell to the shop chimed, she and Garrison disappeared to take care of the new customers.

I turned to Hollister. "You didn't tell her why I was here."

He shrugged. "Her ordeal with her ex and the Magical Task Force has left her with some PTSD. I figured it was better to just let her think you're working on a special spell for an event than to bring up anything that might be a trigger."

Kiera's ex had been an agent with the Magical Task Force and had used his position and power to not only make her life a living hell, but to also frame her for a crime she didn't commit. She'd killed him in self-defense and she'd bear those scars for years to come.

"I can understand that." I pulled out Charlotte's ruby heart ring and a picture I found of her and Minx that Charlotte had taken in one of those coin-operated photo booths. She'd had a number of them, but I brought this one because Charlotte was wearing the eye talisman. The last item was a candle she kept beside her bed that she lit each night. "I hope these are okay. The coven tried a finding spell, but we couldn't get it to work. They think it's because of the black magic."

Hollister nodded. "That's likely."

"Is that going to be a problem for us?" I asked, not sure

what he could do if the black magic was blocking us from seeing Charlotte.

"No." He walked over to a cabinet and pulled out a black mortar and pestle, plus a bag of herbs and a white crystal. "Moonstone," he said. "It helps to provide clarity."

"I could use plenty of that."

"I think that's a universal truth." He walked over to a small round table and put the mortar and pestle in the middle. "Take these," he said, handing me the bag of herbs and the moonstone.

Standing there in his back room, I watched Hollister morph from respectable shop owner to something that was more akin to a mad scientist. He put on a pair of wire-rimmed glasses, rolled up his sleeves, and ran a hand through his styled hair, making it stand on end.

I grinned at him.

"What?"

"That cloak would complete your look right now."

"Stop busting my balls and get over here." He pointed to the spot next to him.

I did as I was told.

"Now, where's that dagger of yours?" he asked.

I opened my bag and was surprised to see that although I hadn't touched it yet, it had turned electric blue and seemed to be pulsing with magic. It had done that before when we were searching for Kiera, but not since. It only glowed when I was touching it. "It's glowing on its own again."

Hollister peered at it and nodded. "The store is charged with a lot of magic. I'd be surprised if it wasn't."

That was why he'd wanted me to come to him. We'd

have better success in his store than we would even at the coven circle. "Okay, tell me what to do."

"I want you to sit there." He pointed to a stool in the middle of the workroom.

"Okay." I took a seat and watched as he drew a pentagram around me using chalk. Once he was done, he placed a circle of candles around me and took the bag of herbs I'd been holding. "Give me a minute to prepare the herbs, and then we'll get started."

I felt a little bit uneasy while I watched Hollister work. He was the mad scientist, and I was the test subject. He was one hundred percent in control of this spell he was going to cast, and I was merely the vessel. It was disconcerting giving someone that much power over what was going to happen next.

"You need to relax, Marion," Hollister said, eyeing me. "If you're going to channel Charlotte's energy, you need to be open to it."

"I'm open to it," I said.

He chuckled. "You look about as open as a fireproof safe."

"That's ridiculous," I said, shaking my head. "I'm here, aren't I?"

"Your body is. But this will only work if you open your heart and mind to finding Charlotte. Can you do that?"

I nodded with no hesitation. At that point, I was certain she was being held against her will, and I'd do whatever it took to find her.

"Good. Now fix your gaze on the moonstone. I'm going

to chant the spell, and you should be able to see her in the flat surface."

"Okay. I'm ready."

"Wait." He reached for my dagger and put it in my free hand and then arranged Charlotte's personal items on the floor around the stool I was sitting on.

Magic pulsed in time with the beat of my heart, and when I looked at the moonstone, it had turned transparent and had smoke swirling inside. My heart started to beat faster. Could this actually work?

Hollister stood on the other side of the pentagram, his arms raised out to the side as he chanted in Latin. His voice rose and fell in time with my heartbeat, and suddenly nothing else existed except for the two of us and the magic filling the pentagram.

"Focus on the moonstone!" Hollister ordered.

My gaze snapped back to the stone in my hand. As soon as it did, magic shot from my dagger, through my body, and straight into the rock that had turned so warm that holding it was almost unbearable.

But then I saw it.

The house. I recognized it immediately, even though I'd never been there. My mother had shown me pictures of it often enough throughout the years. I'd come to hate that house because it represented all the trauma I'd suffered as a result of my mother leaving us.

It was a small compound, surrounded by redwoods on three sides, right on the edge of the Pacific Ocean. The white house stood tall in the filtered sunlight, and right there on the front porch was the woman I'd always suspected was at the heart of Charlotte's disappearance.

Our mother, Liana Adler.

Charlotte was sitting next to her, staring off into the distance.

My mother's voice pierced the air. "Charlotte, just trust him. He knows what he's doing."

Charlotte's voice was flat when she asked, "How can I trust him? Or you?" She turned her cold, angry gaze on Liana. "I'd rather be in prison than let either of you help me."

The door opened, and Denver strode out. There was a large bruise on his right cheek.

Charlotte's gaze tracked him, but she didn't say anything. Neither did he.

It was my mother who finally spoke. "He won't let either of you leave until you sign the contract. Trust me. I know. It's not worth throwing your life away by being stubborn."

There was a long pause before Charlotte finally said, "Go to hell."

CHAPTER 21

$\mathcal{T}$he magic vanished and the moonstone turned solid, leaving me speechless as I tried to process what I'd just witnessed.

"Marion?" Hollister asked. "Are you okay?"

I shook my head, my mouth hanging open like some sort of idiot.

"Did you recognize that house?" he asked.

"Yes." I nodded almost numbly. "It's Arlo Ray's house. Charlotte's biological father."

"She's being held against her will," he said, his voice shaking with fury.

"So is Denver," I said, positive that I'd gotten that right. Between the bruise and my mother telling them neither of them could leave until they signed some sort of contract, I was convinced they were both prisoners. But did my mother have her freedom? I thought she might since she seemed to know something about the way Arlo worked.

"We should call Brix," Hollister said.

"Yeah," I said, hoping it was the right call. I still didn't have proof that Charlotte was innocent of using black magic, but if we could at least get Charlotte home, Sebastian could be appointed her lawyer and she'd be free of her sperm donor and our mother, who once again seemed to be choosing a man over her own daughter. Anger burned brightly in my chest, making me rub the area just over my heart.

Hollister picked up his phone and tapped the buttons, calling Brix. Hollister worked with the Magical Task Force on updating their magical weapons and decommissioning those they seized, so he also had a direct line to Brix and other agents who used his services. A second later, the phone was on speaker, the ring filling the room.

It went straight to voice mail.

"Dammit, Brix," I said into the phone. "My sister is being held against her will, and I think I know who cursed her with black magic. Call either me or Hollister back as soon as possible."

Hollister ended the call. "Should I contact someone else at the agency?"

I shook my head. "I don't trust anyone else. I'm still working on the theory that someone cursed her with black magic, but if it's something else, I could be giving her up to the Magical Task Force. I don't want to give them anything else that could get her into more trouble."

"All right. Then it's just you and me. Let me load up some weapons, and we'll go get your sister."

I gaped at him. "You're going to run headfirst into the lion's den, just to help my sister?"

He nodded. "You were there every step of the way to help my sister-in-law. I'll be here every step of the way to help you find your sister."

Throughout my life, I'd had many friends. A few of them were like family, the ones who'd lay down their lives for me. I hadn't realized until that very moment that Hollister was one of them. I grabbed his hand and squeezed. "Thank you."

"No need for that, but you're welcome." He turned and started rummaging around in his supplies. When he was done, he slung a backpack over his shoulder and said, "Let's go."

THE MOMENT we were in the car I called Sebastian, hoping he could supply me with Arlo's address. I knew what town it was in and had seen it in a few photos that my mother had, but I hadn't actually been there. If we didn't get an address, we'd waste precious time driving around until we found the house.

"Marion, I was just getting ready to call you."

My heart stopped. "You have the background check on Denver?"

"I do. It's a doozy."

"I want to hear it all, but first, I was hoping for a favor," I said. "I need the address for Arlo Ray in Brimstone Bay."

"That's easy. I have it right here," he said. "That's who Denver has been working for since last year."

The information surprised me a little. Since I was pretty sure Denver was being kept against his will, I had questions about why he'd been in Premonition Pointe. Had he been forced to get close to Charlotte? Is that why he'd been in Hallucinations that night?

He rattled off the address and then said, "Tell me you aren't going to charge in there by yourself."

"Okay, I'm not."

"Are you telling me the truth?" he asked, sounding skeptical.

I chuckled. "Yes. Hollister is with me."

"Is there anything I can say that will make you rethink your plan?"

"No. My mother is there, too. I need to find out why they are holding my sister against her will."

"You know I'm going to tell Gigi and the rest of the coven, right?"

I hadn't thought of that, but I wasn't going to ask him to keep what I planned to do a secret from his fiancée. "You don't need to do that."

"Yes, I do," Sebastian said. "Do you have any idea how pissed Gigi would be if she found out I knew her newest coven sister was running straight into a hornets' nest and didn't bother to tell her?"

Yeah, I'd be pissed if Jax kept anything like that from me, too. "Do what you have to do, but please tell them that Hollister and I aren't going in empty-handed. Hollister has us covered. All I plan to do is get my sister out of there and leave."

"I'll tell them, but you know how that goes." He let out a

barely audible sigh. "Be careful, Marion. You don't know what you're walking into."

"Any hints? What is Denver's job title? What does he do for Arlo?"

"He appears to be an apprentice for Arlo's business."

"An apprentice for a restaurant supply business owner?" I asked, certain that wasn't what Denver was doing. When he'd filled out the information at the agency, he'd said he was an artist who had his own business.

"That's what the intel says, but it's probably safe to say that Arlo isn't exactly in the restaurant supply business. There are strong indications that his business is laundering money. We haven't figured out how he's making that money yet, but we're working on it. It looks like something computer related. So be careful, okay?"

"We will. Thanks, Sebastian." I ended the call and set up the GPS. In one hour and twenty-three minutes, Arlo Ray and Liana Adler were going to have to face one pissed-off witch. And maybe this time they'd have to answer for everything they'd done to hurt two women who'd asked for nothing but to be loved.

CHAPTER 22

"This is it," I said, pointing to the left where a gate blocked the driveway.

Hollister pulled in, and after lowering his window, he pressed the intercom.

"No soliciting," the voice on the other end said.

"We're here to see Charlotte Ray," he said, his voice firm but pleasant.

I had serious doubts we were going to be granted entry, but to my astonishment, the gate opened.

Hollister gave me a surprised look and pulled down the drive. We drove through a thicket of trees until the drive opened up to a large parking area in front of the big white house that was framed by the Pacific Ocean. The house was a large Victorian with a lot of character, and it didn't look like anything Arlo Ray would own. It was far too warm and inviting.

"Nice place," Hollister said with a whistle.

"Too nice for Arlo," I said, not hiding my distaste.

"Your mother said you'd show up here," a man with a raspy voice said from the end of the large porch.

I turned and there he was. The villain of our family story. Arlo Ray leaned against one of the pillars, his hands in his pockets and his legs crossed at the ankle. He pushed off the pillar and walked to the edge of the porch.

"I always thought we'd meet sooner, Marion," he said, his lips twisted almost into a sneer.

"Why?" I asked, genuinely curious. "You didn't want anything to do with your own biological daughter. Why would you want to meet her half sister?"

"You're Liana's daughter," he said as if that was obvious.

I shook my head, not caring one bit about this topic. I'd never wanted to meet Arlo. In fact, I'd spent a significant amount of my life pretending he didn't exist. "I'm here to see Charlotte. Can you tell her I'm here?"

"She already knows." He glanced up at one of the windows above him.

There was movement at the window, but the sun shone in such a way that seeing inside was nearly impossible.

"Can you please tell her to come down?" I asked politely.

"She'll come down if she wants to," he said with a shrug.

The door swung open, and instead of Charlotte appearing, my mother strode out, a big smile on her face. "Marion! What a pleasant surprise."

I scowled at her. "Pleasant? I'm guessing you thought I'd never figure out that you were in cahoots with Arlo."

"Cahoots?" she asked with a laugh as if I were the funniest person on the planet. "Please. Arlo called to tell me that Charlotte was here right after you and I spoke this morning, so I immediately made the trip down. It's been a stressful week with the arrest and all. She just really needed her mother."

I coughed, barely covering when I muttered, "Bullshit."

My mother's smile faded and her eyes narrowed slightly when she looked at Hollister. "You haven't introduced us to your companion, Marion. Where are your manners?"

I rolled my eyes. "I guess we'll never know." I waved a hand at my friend. "This is Hollister. Hollister, this is my mother, Liana Adler, and Arlo Ray. He's Charlotte's biological father."

"Hello, Hollister," my mother said with a tight smile.

Arlo snorted. "No need to be polite to him, Liana. He's not here to make friends."

"Talk about forgetting your manners," I said, not bothering to hide my sarcasm. "But Arlo's right. He's here to help me take Charlotte home."

"I'm not coming," Charlotte said and then opened the screen door. Her face was pale, and she had dark circles under her eyes. It was obvious she hadn't been sleeping. Her coloring suggested she wasn't eating either.

"I know you want to," I said softly to her. "Minx misses you."

Charlotte winced, and a single tear rolled silently down her cheek. She ignored it and shook her head. "I can't, Marion. My place is here."

"No it isn't." I wanted to run up onto that porch, grab her, and force her to go with me and Hollister. But I wasn't naive. Everything about this scene screamed that Arlo was either forcing her to stay or had threatened her with something important. "Your place is with me, working at the agency. Partners, remember?"

Pain flashed through her green eyes, and as she stared at me, she seemed to silently plead with me not to make this harder on her.

There was no chance of that. I would not give up on her. I held my hand out to her. "Whatever's happened over the last week, we'll work it out. Sebastian is ready and waiting to take on your case."

"Charlotte has a lawyer," my mother said. "There's no reason to hire someone."

I didn't bother telling her that Sebastian wouldn't take money from us under any circumstances. He protected the coven and their loved ones like they were one of his own, because they were. If any of the coven was in trouble, he'd do whatever he could to help because it was important to Gigi. Charlotte wasn't a coven member, but she was my sister, and they wouldn't sit around and let anything bad happen to her if they could help it.

"I spoke with Eli," I said, just trying to keep my sister talking. "He's waiting for you to get home."

Charlotte blinked at me, seemingly confused, then her shoulders slumped. "He probably just needs me to cure his… issues."

"That's true, but I think he'd still like to talk to you," I said.

She slowly shook her head. "There's work to do here."

"Like what?" Nausea started to take over as I thought

about the scene I'd witnessed in the moonstone. "You didn't sign any contract with Arlo, did you?"

"Not yet, but..." She sucked in a sharp breath. "It's better for everyone if I do."

The door swung open and Denver strode out, anger etched all over his face. "No, it isn't." He turned to Arlo and out of nowhere, he blasted his boss with magic, sending the guy flying off the porch and into a towering redwood tree.

"Denver!" Liana shouted and ran toward him, her own magic flying. Denver held a hand up, deflecting her attack, sending the magic back in her direction. She dove behind a wooden chair and screamed when it shattered.

"Go!" Denver pushed Charlotte toward us. "Go now and never look back."

"I'm not leaving you here with them," Charlotte said defiantly. "You know I won't."

He opened his mouth to say something, but Liana jumped out from behind the broken chair and stepped in front of Charlotte. Her entire body was shaking with fury. "Denver, go back inside."

Denver stood there, sweat covering his face while his entire body shook as if he were fighting off an invisible attack.

"What's happening right now?" I demanded, striding up to my mother. "What are you doing to Denver?"

"Nothing. He works for Arlo, and part of his contract is to do what the two of us say. If I say go inside, he has to go inside," she said and pressed her lips into a thin line as she scowled at the man.

Denver's feet started to shuffle in the direction of the house, but he was fighting it every step of the way.

"Contracts were made to be broken," Hollister said right before he leaped onto the porch. Using one of his small daggers, he clipped the necklace Denver was wearing, causing the tree pendant to fall onto the porch.

Smoke billowed from the place where the pendant landed, and suddenly there was a fire raging on the wooden deck.

Someone screamed. I thought it was my mother. Then all three of them, Hollister, Charlotte, and Denver, were next to me with Hollister ordering us all to leave immediately.

We'd only gotten about ten feet when Arlo's voice boomed from the smoke. "Stop!"

Charlotte and Denver stopped in their tracks while Hollister and I tried to drag them along.

"Nobody will be leaving here today," Arlo said with a growl as he emerged from the smoke and used his magic to extinguish the fire.

"You've lost your mind, old man," I said. "Hollister and I will leave anytime we want to."

"Really?" He glanced down at our feet. "I'd like to see you try."

I tried to lift my foot, to move forward, to move *anywhere*, but it was as if my feet had been trapped in concrete. No matter what I tried to do, I just stood there, helpless.

Hollister appeared to be having the same problem.

"Now, I think it's time we had a chat. Charlotte, Denver, go inside. I'll have instructions for you in a few hours."

Both of them immediately turned and slipped into the house, letting the door slam behind them.

"You've compelled them to do what you ask," I accused Arlo. "You're holding your own daughter captive. For what? A few more dollars to add to your bank account? You're the worst kind of human. The kind who only cares about money and power. It's disgusting."

"Disgusting or not, this is who I am," he said mildly. "It just so happens that the bond is stronger when you're blood related, so getting Charlotte on board wasn't much of a problem. All it took was a few sleepless nights and an effective potion. Now she does what I ask, usually without questions. But you're here now, causing problems, so I have some choices to make."

"The only choice to make is to let Charlotte go before the entire Magical Task Force comes calling. What do you think is going to happen when they come looking for us and find that you've been cursing people with black magic to do your bidding?"

He raised one eyebrow. "Black magic, huh? What makes you think I have to stoop so low in order to get my employees to follow my directions?"

"Because you're a bastard?" I asked, taunting him.

"It's sure going to be a shame when they come looking for you and Charlotte tells them you accidentally slipped on the rocks and died instantly of a head injury." A sickly-sweet smile claimed his lips. "It's always a tragedy when someone dies."

DEANNA CHASE

"Arlo!" Liana admonished. "That's my daughter you're talking about."

Oh, now she was defending me? It took until he'd actually threatened to kill me before she spoke up? At least it was good to know she had *some* boundaries.

"She's threatening me, Liana. You know I won't stand for that," Arlo said, his gaze so cold it made me shiver despite the warm afternoon.

"You will not kill my daughter," Liana told him, her voice full of fire. "Put her under contract if you have to, but if you harm her, you'll have to answer to me."

Arlo laughed. "Answer to you? You've lost your goddamned mind."

"You married this man?" I asked my mother, unable to believe that she'd leave my father for this trash. "What were you thinking?"

"I'm trying to help you, Marion. Now isn't the time for your smart mouth or your judgment about matters you know nothing about." She stalked over to Arlo, magic sparking in her palms.

Arlo glanced down and let out a low chuckle. "You know I always did like it when you got assertive. It makes the bedroom activities so much more interesting."

"I'm not fucking with you this time, Arlo," Liana said. "Hurt my daughter and I'll rip your fucking throat out."

Arlo's eyes twinkled with interest as he watched her move closer. When she was finally right in front of him, he grabbed the back of her hair, fisting it and then kissing her hard. When he finally let her up for air, she was breathing heavily and staring at him in a lust haze.

216

"For fuck's sake," I ground out, still unable to move my feet. "How long are you going to leave us trapped here? Until you're done getting each other off?"

"Marion." Liana shook her head. "Don't be crass."

My chest was tight, and the anger directed at her was so overwhelming I thought I might explode right there in the front yard. There'd be no need for anyone to kill me. I'd already be in a million pieces.

"Your husband, or boyfriend, or whatever he is these days is talking about killing me, and you're worried about me being crass?" I asked her incredulously. "I knew you were awful, but I never realized it was *this* bad."

"You'd better start respecting me," Liana said. "I'm the only thing between you and Arlo right now. If I step aside, he'll either kill you or force you into a ninety-nine-year contract with him where you will do whatever is asked of you with no opportunity to leave. Do you understand what I'm telling you?"

"Let me guess. That you both suck, and if Hollister and I don't find a way out of this mess ourselves, you'll spend eternity telling me it's all my fault because I showed up to help my sister?"

"You're an ungrateful brat," my mother said, crossing her arms over her chest. Then she looked over at Arlo and said, "Do what you have to do."

CHAPTER 23

"*Y*ou bitch!" Charlotte appeared out of nowhere, launching herself at our mother. They both went down in a heap of arms and legs, rolling around in the garden beds in front of the porch.

Arlo growled and said, "Charlotte, stop!"

My sister immediately froze. She was still on top of our mother, pinning her down, but she was no longer trying to restrain her.

"I can't believe you attacked me," our mother said to Charlotte as if she hadn't been party to the last twenty minutes of threats and promises.

"I can't believe you're such a worthless parent," Charlotte spat in her face. "Did you know I used to ask about you every night after you left?"

Liana shook her head but looked more curious than horrified that she'd left an eight-year-old behind.

"Marion spent a lot of time soothing me so that I didn't

cry myself to sleep," Charlotte said. "Do you know that she never once said a bad thing about you? Not back then, anyway. You owe her a debt. Instead, you've basically turned her over to a monster, just like you did to me when you had Denver bring me back here after I was arrested."

"Our mom is responsible for this?" I choked out, horrified. I'd known she was trying to convince Charlotte to sign Arlo's contract, but I hadn't realized she was in so deep that she was actually bringing him her children for a sacrifice.

"She's evil," Charlotte cried.

Liana pushed her off and got to her feet. She stared down at her youngest daughter and shook her head sadly. "All I wanted to do was try to warn you to stay away. To live your life and stay far away from me and Arlo, but instead, the two of you shunned me. Refused to meet with me when I had a window to warn you and tell you to get rid of that damned talisman that Arlo gave you on the yacht. Instead, you and your ungrateful sister couldn't make any time for me. And now look." She waved a hand at Arlo, who was glaring at her. "You're stuck. He'll either bind you to him or kill you." She glanced back at me. "Your choice."

"That's a hell of a choice, *Mom*," I said. "We've got the mother of the fucking year right here, don't you think, Charlotte?"

My sister grunted.

"My thoughts exactly." My feet were starting to come back to life, and I was certain that Arlo's spell was beginning to wear off.

Hollister, who was still standing next to me, nudged my

arm and then slipped a cool glass bottle into my hand. I glanced down, seeing a red potion inside the small vial.

"When I say now," he whispered, "throw it as hard as you can at Arlo."

I gave him the tiniest of nods. I was through with this particular brand of family crazy.

Charlotte was still lying on the ground, barely moving while our mother glared at me.

"You brought this on yourself," Liana started.

But Hollister cut her off, yelling, "Now!"

I threw the bottle of red potion at Arlo, hitting him square in the chest. He glanced down at it, seemingly in disbelief. He immediately raised his arms, his fingers pointing right at me.

Hollister threw his batch of potion and cried, "Neutralize!"

Magic sparked around Arlo, lighting up his arms, hands, and face, only to vanish a second later, leaving him standing in shadows, shivering as if all the blood had been drained from his system.

Arlo collapsed into the dirt and rasped, "Help."

Liana charged us, and a second later, the front door slammed open with Denver following her lead as Charlotte pushed herself up from the ground.

Magic poured from my mom, hitting Hollister right in the chest. Denver went for him next, pouncing on him and quickly tying him up with zip ties.

That left Charlotte. Her magic was swirling around her, flashing red, indicating her anger had taken over. She likely didn't have any limits if she was mad and programmed to attack anyone who tried to take out Arlo.

"Charlotte!" I demanded. "Stop this. This isn't you. Fight off that compulsion and we'll get you home where you belong."

She let out a maniacal laugh. "You think it works that way? As long as he's alive, I'm bound to him. It's our blood. I'm his daughter. I can never escape him now. All that will happen if I disobey is that he'll kill the people I love. You shouldn't have come here, Marion. It isn't safe for you. Either leave now, or I will be forced to kill you." The last two words were full of pain as she warned me. "Do you understand? I can't control this. There's no way to end it now that he's put it in motion. My life is over, but yours doesn't need to be. Go, please, Marian. Live your life for me and take care of Minx."

She sniffled as the tears rolled freely now.

I reached out, taking her hand in mine. She was right. Her magic felt different now. Heavier. Full of regret.

All I wanted to do was help her shed the shackles that Arlo had put on her magic. Free her from these toxic people, take her home, and show her that she had many happy years ahead of her. "I won't leave you!" I cried as I pulled my dagger out of the holder at my side. Magic poured into me and straight into her.

We lit up like the sun right there in front of Arlo's house, shining like a beacon of pure goodness.

Arlo pushed up from his place in the dirt, watching us with hatred in his gaze.

"Stay down, old man," I ordered, feeling the magic

combining with my sister's and filling my soul. "Or we'll end you right now."

He staggered to his feet and pulled his own dagger from a side pocket. It was more sinister than mine, with a jagged edge meant to do serious harm.

I wasn't deterred. With Charlotte by my side, I'd never felt more powerful.

"Come at us, Arlo. I dare you," I challenged.

"Marion, no!" a group of familiar voices sounded in the distance, but I was too far gone. Too ready to end Arlo and the hold he had on my sister. This was it, either me or him, because I wasn't leaving there without Charlotte completely free of him and his sick games.

Arlo charged, his arm steady and magic aimed straight for my heart.

"No!" Charlotte cried and lunged in front of me, taking the hit of his magic right in her chest.

Charlotte froze, Arlo's magic trying and failing to pierce the magical barrier we'd created together. Our magic was protecting her, but it was also obvious that as long as she was under attack, moving wasn't an option.

I had to take Arlo down, or Charlotte would be stuck there until one of us ran out of magic.

Gripping my sister's hand tightly, I raised my dagger and lunged for him, aiming for his shoulder. Arlo turned right at the last second, trying to block my dagger with his, making them collide.

The two daggers were pressed against each other with magic bouncing off both, sending sparks everywhere.

I stared into Arlo's eyes and with every last bit of

strength left in me, I said, "Go to hell, old man." Then I focused on his dagger and watched as he ever so slowly pulled back and then stabbed himself right in the gut.

Standing over him, I watched as he collapsed, blood running from the wound in his gut.

"No!" our mother cried and ran to him. "Arlo? Don't you dare die on me," she said through her tears. "You can't leave me like this. I can't take the fall for all your sins!"

"Ms. Adler?" Brix said, appearing out of nowhere.

"He's dying," she said, staring up at Brix with vacant eyes.

"You need to move aside. The paramedics will take care of him now," Brix said as he flashed his badge. "I'm sorry to inform you that you are under arrest for aiding and abetting a black magic user."

As Brix read our mother her rights, I turned to Charlotte, still holding her hand. "Are you okay?"

Tears streamed down her face as she shook her head. But before I could ask anything else, she grabbed me in a bear hug and held on for dear life.

Eventually she said, "You came for me."

"Of course I did," I said. "You're my sister."

She buried her face in my shoulder and sobbed. Over her shoulder, I spotted Denver sitting on the porch, his head between his legs as he struggled to breathe. Hollister was sitting beside him, talking to him softly.

And just to the side of the porch, I spotted all six of my coven members. They'd drawn a pentagram, built a fire ring, and were conducting some sort of ritual. Inside the fire ring, I spotted a number of daggers, some pendants, and even a couple of crystals. It wasn't long before I realized they were performing a cleansing ritual. It was what was done when witches wanted to strip cursed objects of their power but also preserve the items.

Brix had likely asked them to perform the ritual before he transported the items to the Magical Task Force for evidence.

A truck pulled into the parking area, and Jax jumped out. He ran over to me, and although I still had my arm around Charlotte's shoulder, he pulled me into a hug, clutching me to him. "You were supposed to call me before you ran head first into something like this, remember?"

I nodded and blinked back tears. I was just too overwhelmed to say anything. I'd nearly killed a man using my magic, and then my mother had been arrested. I still didn't know what Arlo was doing that required him to have witches on staff who were compelled to do anything he asked. All I knew was that when he stabbed himself, the blood he'd shed by his own hand had broken the spell. It was enough for now.

CHAPTER 24

"Are you sure you two don't want to come work for the Magical Task Force?" Brix asked me and Charlotte.

We were at his office for the second day in a row, answering questions so that he could close his case against Charlotte. Once it had become clear that Arlo had been the one to spell her and then bind it with his talismans, it hadn't taken long to get the black magic charges dropped.

There was still an investigation around the accidental curse she'd cast at Hallucinations, but Brix had offered to drop it if we found a way to help every person who was cursed that day. Charlotte had readily agreed.

"I wish more than anything that had never happened," she said. "If I could take it back, I would. The only thing left to do is move forward and make it right for all of them."

"It's not really your fault. You know that, right?" Brix

asked her. "You didn't know that you were channeling black magic. How could you?"

She gritted her teeth. "I should've known not to trust Arlo that night my mother took me to meet him. I took the talismans because he insisted. If I'd just walked out, maybe we wouldn't be here. Maybe our mother might not be facing nine months in jail. Maybe… Hell, I don't know."

"Because of you, Denver has his freedom back," I said. "If you hadn't shown up, he'd never have been successful in breaking the binding Arlo had over him."

"It's because of you," my sister insisted. "Without you, none of us would've led a normal life again."

"You'd have found a way," I said, giving her hand a squeeze.

Brix shook his head at us. "You two make a great team. That magic you harness together would be a huge asset to the Magical Task Force. Think about it, okay?"

"I don't want to hunt bad witches," I said.

Charlotte bit down on her bottom lip as she looked at me, her eyes full of compassion. "We can't just walk away from people in need, Marion. What if you hadn't come along? What would my life look like then?"

I stared at her, my mouth hanging open a little. "Are you saying you want to work for the MTF?"

"No. I'm saying I don't want anyone else to go through what we did." She placed one of her hands over one of mine. The magic flared to life and glowed, lighting up the gray room. "We have this gift. I think we should use it."

"Jax and Denver won't like it," I said and then chuckled. "That would never stop either of us though."

"Nope," she said and then turned to Brix. "Can we work on a case-by-case basis like you do?"

He frowned as he thought it over. "If you worked for me, we could do the case-by-case thing. If you worked with another agent, I'm guessing you'd have to be a little more flexible."

"I'll do it if we only work with you," I said.

"Only me?" His brows shot up.

"I don't trust anyone else," I said with a shrug. "And I won't let my sister be used as a pawn by this agency."

Brix gave me a slow smile. "I always did like you, Marion Matched. Now I admire you. That's exactly what I said when they asked me to go back to work for them. I'll get the paperwork ready to go, and then we'll talk about what's coming up next."

"I still have a business to run," I warned him.

"*We* have a business to run," Charlotte corrected.

I snorted. "I see you didn't forget I said that."

"Nope. It was my magic being controlled, not my brain." She smiled sweetly at me.

Pride surged through me. Charlotte had come back into my life appearing to be shallow, a tad lazy, and somewhat lost on where and what she wanted to be. Now she was fully committed to living in Premonition Pointe, working with me at the agency, and being my partner in magic when the Magical Task Force needed us.

She'd also told me that her and Denver's romance was on hold indefinitely. While their auras were still a strong match, neither of them were ready to deal with what they'd gone through during the time they were with Arlo.

Especially Denver. He'd been there months and had been forced to spell many of Arlo's visitors into forgetting they'd ever been there. He'd also been instructed to steal their credit cards and any cash they had to enrich Arlo.

The one thing that really put the final nail in the coffin of the two of them pursuing any kind of relationship was the fact that Arlo had sent Denver to woo Charlotte. That's why he was at Hallucinations that night. He'd been there spying on Charlotte on Arlo's orders. Arlo had wanted them in a relationship because then it would be easier for him to control both of them. Neither Charlotte nor Denver were ready to unpack what it meant that their relationship started off as a lie.

As it turned out, Arlo had been smuggling illegal aliens over the border for money and then selling them off to the highest bidders who would then practically enslave them while they worked farms and warehouses at a ridiculously low rate. His clients raked in the cash since they never had to deal with payroll, and Arlo took a cut of their profits. He'd also dabbled in drug running and selling other items on the black market, always compelling his minions to do his dirty work while he sat in his office pretending he was a corporate genius.

It was easy to make money when you had free labor and no morals.

Arlo was going to recover from his gut wound, but he'd be incarcerated when the hospital released him while he awaited his trial. The chances were high that he'd be locked up for decades with little to no chance of ever being released.

"I have everything I need," Brix said. "Go home. Get some rest. Find your clients their dream partners and then one day soon you'll be hearing from me. Got it?"

I saluted him. "Got it, Director Brix."

He rolled his eyes at me. "Get out before I call security."

"We're going," I said with a laugh. "Just don't call us as soon as we get home. It's family night."

"I'll try my best," he said and waved us out of his office.

On our way out, I said, "Char?"

"Yeah?"

"Have I told you how much I love it that you're my sister?"

Charlotte stopped and stared at me. "Have you been drinking?"

I blinked at her. "No. Why?"

"I nearly got you trapped in a never-ending nightmare. You can't really be glad I came back into your life."

Clearing my throat, I met her gaze and said, "Char, that crap can happen to any witch at any time. It's not the first time I was certain some jackass was going to do me in. That always sucks. But the difference is, I'm coming out of this ordeal with a best friend, a sister, and a business partner all wrapped up in one tidy package. And we're both stronger for it. I don't regret that."

"Fucking hell, Marion. You're gonna make me cry... again." She wiped at her teary eyes and laughed when she sniffed. Then she turned to me, a serious expression on her face. "I love you, too, big sis. But if my dog has abandoned me for good for that boyfriend of yours, we're gonna have words."

"As we should." I winked at her and was still smiling to myself as we climbed into my SUV.

CHAPTER 25

"*D*rink up!" I encouraged Jax. "It's an engagement party. We're supposed to be celebrating." We were at Carly Preston's house to celebrate Damon Grant's engagement to his longtime boyfriend, who no one, not even insiders like Carly, had known about.

He'd kept it secret to protect his career, but after being out of work for weeks while his ankle healed, something had changed and he'd decided to come out, at least to his friends and the producers of the movie. They'd responded by making his character gay, saying they'd always wanted the script that way but that his agent had insisted he'd never go for it. Now he was thrilled to be representing his community and doing it in a very positive film.

Charlotte and I had kept our promise, and after two weeks of trying to get in to see Damon, he'd finally granted us access. We'd cleared up the acne and any bedroom performance issues quickly, but the ankle hadn't been a direct result of the curse, so there was nothing we could do to help other than offer our apologies. He'd been gracious, thanked us, and then promptly asked us to come back and visit him while he was laid up in town. So for the past six weeks, we'd visited once a month, played cards, learned about the film industry, and become pretty good friends with the normally reclusive movie star.

Jax glanced down at Minx, who was curled up in the sling against his chest. "Minx doesn't care for all the people."

I rolled my eyes. "You could have left her at home. She doesn't mind the crate we got her."

"No, I couldn't," he insisted. "You know how she's been since Charlotte got back. Clingy, destructive, lots of anxiety. Leaving her home by herself just wasn't an option. I wouldn't have been able to stand it when there's no reason she couldn't come and hang out with me."

It was true. Minx had been having some issues. The vet thought it was separation anxiety from when Charlotte was gone. The two were practically inseparable now, but any time Charlotte left the house without her, Minx sort of lost her shit. We'd started taking her to the office with us, which was fine. But on nights like tonight when we were all out celebrating, it was more of a challenge.

Ty walked up to us with a glass of champagne in his hand. He seemed a little antsy, and I wondered what that was about. But before I could ask, Charlotte appeared holding a red gift bag.

I pointed to the gift table, but Charlotte shook her head. "This is for Jax from Minx."

Jax frowned. "What?"

"She wanted to get you a gift, and it took us a bit of time to find it. We had to order it and it just came today." She handed the bag to him. "Go on. Open it, and then I'll put it in the car so you won't have to hold it."

Jax glanced down at Minx, who was looking at him a little smugly. Or at least that's what it looked like to me, since she'd gotten what she wanted when Jax had decided to bring her with him. Those, two. I swear, I'd never seen anything like it. They'd gone from mortal enemies to besties in what seemed like two seconds flat. "We're stealing the spotlight, Minx," Jax told the dog. "The gifts should be for the guests of honor, not the dog sitter," he said, his tone sweet and full of love.

"Go on. Show us what it is," I said, impatient to find out what a dog got her favorite human. Or at least her second favorite after Charlotte.

Jax reached in and pulled out a pair of jeans. Not just any jeans, though, I thought when I spotted the label. They were the exact same brand and style that Minx ruined that morning when she'd torn his pants.

"Minx, you got these for me?" Jax cooed, making me cringe just a little. As sweet as it was that he loved her so much, some days it was a little over the top. Like right now.

Or maybe I was just a little jealous.

Of a dog.

Hey, I just wanted to be wrapped up against my boyfriend, but right now it'd have to wait because Minx was hogging my spot.

"Thanks, Charlotte," Jax said, giving her a grateful smile. "You didn't have to do this, but I appreciate the gesture."

"You're very welcome," she said and then turned to me. "Why are you scowling?"

"I'm scowling?" I asked.

"Yeah, like you can't believe I gave your boyfriend pants." She frowned. "What's going on?"

I laughed. "Nothing. Nothing at all. Just wishing I was Minx right now. Lucky bitch."

Charlotte laughed along with me. "Pathetic."

"Speaking of pathetic..." I nodded across the room toward Denver. He'd spent about a month sorting himself out and then moved to Premonition Pointe. He'd since asked Charlotte out twice. She'd turned him down twice, stating she still needed more time to process everything.

But I happened to know that she was ready to date again. I could just tell. She was bored with hanging out with me and Jax. And while Ty and Kennedy had her over a couple nights a week, they couldn't be her only friends and source of entertainment. Plus, they needed their time alone, too. "He's been staring at you," I said.

"I know." She took a large gulp of her champagne.

"Why don't you go talk to him," I said, nudging her in his direction.

"Because, Marion, if I do, you know what's going to happen."

"Is that so bad?" I asked. "It's been weeks. Everyone's curses have been reversed, even your ex who you compelled to do your bidding. You're free. Denver is free. And you two really like each other. What's the harm?"

She closed her eyes and shook her head. "I keep thinking all I'm going to see is Arlo, or his house, or Mom selling us out to her on again-off again husband. Because goddess knows, he was always more important to her than we were."

"What if you just focus on the fact that you both survived a shitty situation and that you're grateful to have it behind you? He was never at fault for any of that. Just like you weren't," I reminded her. "If you want to talk to him, now's a good time. If you don't, that's okay too. I just want you to have some fun. And I think Denver is pretty fun when he isn't cursed. Don't you?"

"Yeah."

"That's what I thought."

Charlotte looked at me, rolled her eyes, and said, "Don't get a big head about this, thinking you're great at matchmaking. I was considering talking to him anyway."

"Of course not." I pressed a hand to my chest. "Now go. Stop making the man wait for you."

As Charlotte strolled across the room, Celia popped into existence.

"It's about time," the ghost said. "She needs to get laid."

Damon Grant and his fiancé were walking by, and Damon, who'd just taken a drink, sputtered, "Celia, where the hell have you been?"

She smiled sweetly at him. "I've been working on my officiating skills. You're going to die when you see me in action."

Kelly Castor stared at Celia wide-eyed and then turned to Damon. "You want a ghost to be our officiant?"

"Sure," Damon said. "She's the one responsible for helping me realize that I didn't need to stay in the closet. It seems appropriate that she be the one to help us make it official."

"Can a ghost even do that?" I asked. "And have it be legal?"

"Marion!" Celia cried. "Stop trying to ruin this for me."

Damon laughed. "No, it's not. That's why Kelly and I already went to the courthouse. We're already official. Celia's officiating will be symbolic."

"Well, isn't that lovely," Celia said and then wiped away a tear.

"Are you crying?" I asked her. "I don't think I've ever seen you do that before."

"Shut up. I can be a softy sometimes," she insisted.

"More than sometimes," Damon said with a wink and then let himself be dragged off to go talk to more guests.

"He's great," I said. "Looks like you made the most of watching over him."

She shrugged one shoulder. "We were both bored, and the next thing I knew, we were telling each other our life stories. I think the story of my death lit a fire under his ass. Kelly owes me one."

"We all do," I said and watched as she flushed.

Since when did ghosts flush? I didn't know, but it was happening now.

"I've got to go," she said and vanished.

I stood at the party, glancing around, and felt my heart swell with happiness when I spotted Charlotte and Denver kissing out on the balcony. Most of the people I loved were at the party. The coven, Jax, my sister, Ty and Kennedy. Even my dad, Tazia, Aunt Lucy, and Gael had been invited.

When I moved to Premonition Pointe, all I'd wanted to do was set up a premier midlife dating agency. I'd done that, but it wasn't the most important thing in my life anymore. Instead, I'd built a family in this small beachside town. A family that filled my heart with a joy I'd never known.

Jax and I were going strong. I finally had the relationship with Charlotte that I'd always hoped was possible when I learned I had a sister. Ty and Kennedy were my boys and they were building a strong life together. Hollister was a good friend I'd gotten a lot closer with. We chatted about spells and potions at least once or twice a week. And sometime next month, the coven was going to perform the formal ritual to induct me into their circle. I hadn't realized how much I was looking forward to it until they'd set the date. Now I could hardly wait.

Life just didn't get any better than this.

My phone buzzed, and I glanced down to see Brix's name flash on the screen.

There was only one sentence and an address. *Emergency, I need my magic duo.*

I quickly put my drink down, made my way out to the balcony, and found Charlotte.

"We're on."

She blinked at me once, then when the words registered, she told Denver she'd call him later and said, "Let's go."

DEANNA'S BOOK LIST

Witches of Keating Hollow:
Soul of the Witch
Heart of the Witch
Spirit of the Witch
Dreams of the Witch
Courage of the Witch
Love of the Witch
Power of the Witch
Essence of the Witch
Muse of the Witch
Vision of the Witch
Waking of the Witch
Honor of the Witch
Promise of the Witch

Witches of Christmas Grove:
A Witch For Mr. Holiday

A Witch For Mr. Christmas
A Witch For Mr. Winter
A Witch For Mr. Mistletoe

Premonition Pointe Novels:

Witching For Grace
Witching For Hope
Witching For Joy
Witching For Clarity
Witching For Moxie
Witching For Kismet

Miss Matched Midlife Dating Agency:

Star-crossed Witch
Honor-bound Witch
Outmatched Witch
Moonstruck Witch

Jade Calhoun Novels:

Haunted on Bourbon Street
Witches of Bourbon Street
Demons of Bourbon Street
Angels of Bourbon Street
Shadows of Bourbon Street
Incubus of Bourbon Street
Bewitched on Bourbon Street
Hexed on Bourbon Street
Dragons of Bourbon Street

Pyper Rayne Novels:

Spirits, Stilettos, and a Silver Bustier
Spirits, Rock Stars, and a Midnight Chocolate Bar
Spirits, Beignets, and a Bayou Biker Gang
Spirits, Diamonds, and a Drive-thru Daiquiri Stand
Spirits, Spells, and Wedding Bells

Ida May Chronicles:
Witched To Death
Witch, Please
Stop Your Witchin'

Crescent City Fae Novels:
Influential Magic
Irresistible Magic
Intoxicating Magic

Last Witch Standing:
Bewitched by Moonlight
Soulless at Sunset
Bloodlust By Midnight
Bitten At Daybreak

Witch Island Brides:
The Wolf's New Year Bride
The Vampire's Last Dance
The Warlock's Enchanted Kiss
The Shifter's First Bite

Destiny Novels:
Defining Destiny

Accepting Fate

Wolves of the Rising Sun:
Jace
Aiden
Luc
Craved
Silas
Darien
Wren

Black Bear Outlaws:
Cyrus
Chase
Cole

Bayou Springs Alien Mail Order Brides:
Zeke
Gunn
Echo

ABOUT THE AUTHOR

New York Times and USA Today bestselling author, Deanna Chase, is a native Californian, who's splits her time between New Orleans and the Pacific Northwest. When she isn't writing, she is often goofing off with her husband, traveling with her besties, or playing with her two shih tzu dogs. For more information and updates on newest releases visit her website at deannachase.com.

Made in United States
Troutdale, OR
02/04/2025

28678962R00152